The Christmas Cottage

THE CHRISTMAS COTTAGE

A Love at Langley Park Romance

JANE PORTER

The Christmas Cottage
Copyright© 2023 Jane Porter
Tule Publishing First Printing, December 2023

The Tule Publishing, Inc.

ALL RIGHTS RESERVED

First Publication by Tule Publishing 2023

Cover design by Lee Hyat Designs at www.LeeHyat.com
Photograph by Gizella Petz at www.gizellapetz.com

No part of this book may be used or reproduced in any manner whatsoever without written permission except in the case of brief quotations embodied in critical articles and reviews.

This is a work of fiction. Names, characters, places, and incidents are products of the author's imagination or are used fictitiously. Any resemblance to actual events, locales, organizations, or persons, living or dead, is entirely coincidental.

AI was not used to create any part of this book and no part of this book may be used for generative training.

ISBN: 978-1-962707-01-5

Dedication

For Meghan,
10 years of Christmas stories
10 years of friendship
10 years of you being an absolute angel—
the gift I never expected

Chapter One

After a twelve-hour flight from Seattle to the United Kingdom, with a two-hour layover at Heathrow, Ella's final flight touched down at the Manchester airport and was taxiing to the gate.

Ella Roberts exhaled, relieved and excited to be on the ground in Manchester, her return flight not for two weeks. For the first time in years, she was taking a proper vacation over the Christmas holidays. Soon, she'd be reunited with her sister, Cara, whom she hadn't seen much since Cara moved to the UK a year ago—with the exception of Cara's gorgeous, intimate August wedding in the San Juan Islands.

Ella was very much looking forward to spending her Christmas holiday with Cara and her husband, Alec, at Langley Park, Alec's ancestral home. She'd be staying in the same stone cottage Cara had last year when she met Alec, a successful, wealthy businessman who spent the majority of his time in London but did return to Derbyshire for the holidays.

Last December, Alec was Viscount Sherbourne, but with his father's death during the late spring, he'd become the

Earl of Sherbourne, making Cara a countess, which amused Ella to no end. Probably because Cara was the least pretentious person Ella knew. Cara was warm and kind. Grounded. She was someone who truly cared about the well-being of others and was no doubt the reason why Alec fell in love with her, despite Cara being American and not a proper wife for an aristocrat. These differences sent Cara home from Langley Park heartbroken last December, but then Alec proved to be a true hero and appeared in Bellingham at the Roberts family home on New Year's Eve to win her back.

It had been a truly romantic gesture and, after a seven and a half month engagement, Alex and Cara married in a lovely American ceremony, and were now hosting a reception at Langley Park for all the friends and families who couldn't make the actual wedding. Ella had come to represent the Robertses, as well as spend time with her much-loved big sister. She probably should have brought her computer with her and done some work. But at the last moment, Ella left it home, determined to relax for the next two weeks. She hadn't felt relaxed in years, not since starting her graduate program. She was a half year away from earning her PhD and she had a heavy schedule of teaching and reading papers, never mind finishing her dissertation, but she didn't have to think about any of that, not until she returned to Bellingham.

The bell chimed on the plane, alerting everyone the aircraft had parked and the seatbelt light went off. Ella rose, gathered her carry-on luggage, and joined the passengers amassing in the aisle. Ella was too happy to be irritable. She was so looking forward to exploring the area with Cara, who had bought tickets for them to tour the great houses, Chatsworth and Haddon Hall, beautifully decorated for Christmas.

It was said that Chatsworth had been Jane Austen's inspiration for Mr. Darcy's Pemberley Hall, and as an English literature scholar specializing in nineteenth-century fiction, specifically gender roles in nineteenth-century fiction written by women, women such as Austen and Alcott, Ella could justify an Austen-focused holiday. Last year, she'd spent time in Boston and Concord Massachusetts where Alcott had lived and later died. It only seemed fair to devote equal time to Jane Austen.

Or, she rationalized as she packed some travel books for sightseeing, if it worked out. If not, the village of Bakewell, an easy walk from Langley Park, would prove to be diverting with all of the holiday decorations.

As the queuing passengers slowly inched forward toward the plane exit, Ella turned her phone on, and checked for reception. Not yet. Cara had warned her it might take a while. Untroubled, Ella put her phone into her pocket, shouldered her backpack and changed hands on her carry-on suitcase. She'd need to collect her large, checked suitcase and then they'd be off. The Manchester airport wasn't far from Langley Park, just an hour if there was no traffic, which meant they'd arrive at Langley Park just after noon and still have all day to talk and explore the house and village.

Ella felt a bubble of happiness fill her. Her luggage appeared quickly, and as she'd cleared customs in Heathrow, it wasn't long until she made her way to arrivals, her gaze sweeping those who'd gathered outside security looking for Cara's shoulder length blonde hair, and there were blondes waiting, but no one that looked remotely like her sister.

She walked more slowly through the throng, still looking for Cara, but wondering if perhaps Alec had come instead. But no, she didn't see Alec, either.

And then she saw her name on a sign. Ella Roberts. Ella looked at the man holding the sign, and her stomach fell. *Baird?*

Adrenaline rushed through her, making her legs weak. Baird MacLauren was the last person she'd expected to see at the airport. She suspected he would be included in the party Alec and Cara were throwing Saturday, but that was still days away.

Heart thudding, she walked toward him, bags heavy, and getting heavier.

They'd had a thing in August, a very brief thing, at Cara and Alec's wedding, culminating in the hottest kiss of her life. She'd heard about intoxicating kisses but had never experienced one, not until the gorgeous, sexy awful Scotsman had shown her just what a kiss should feel like.

Truly, it had been a kiss to end all kisses, the kind of kiss that came after a glass of champagne on the most beautiful summer night. She hadn't fallen in love with him—he'd made sure of that—but those twenty minutes behind the boathouse, in the shadows and moonlight, had made her imagine a life she'd never known, a life with someone who'd passionately love her, a life with marriage, babies—

And that was when he stepped away, and apologized. *Apologized.*

He'd made a mistake.

He asked for her forgiveness.

He'd forgotten himself.

And then worst of all. He wasn't exactly single. Not entirely.

One more apology and then he walked away, and she leaned against the boathouse and fought tears and rage. How dare he kiss her like that when he wasn't available? How dare he make her feel so beautiful only to destroy it all?

She didn't see him the rest of the evening and when she woke up the next day, head aching, eyes gritty from lack of sleep, she discovered he'd taken a water taxi back to Seattle at dawn to make a flight home.

Ella was glad she wouldn't have to see him because she, who dated often and rarely felt anything, realized that she'd come awfully close to falling in love with the Scotsman.

"How was your flight?" Baird asked, closing the distance between them to take her two rolling bags from her.

She nodded, forcing a polite smile. "Uneventful."

"Is this everything?" he asked, gesturing to her suitcases.

She nodded again, avoiding meeting his eyes because she felt foolish with her heart racing and her emotions swirling—so many emotions, unexpected emotions. She'd worked hard to block him from her mind and now he was here, and she felt caught off guard in the worst sort of way. She didn't like feeling so … so everything.

"My car's not far," he said, walking. "But if you'd prefer for me to collect you at the curb?"

"No," she said quickly. "It will feel good to move and stretch my legs."

"It is a long flight," he agreed.

She fell into step walking next to him as he led them through the crowd to the airport exit. She felt his gaze as they stepped outside and wished she could think of something to say, something to fill the silence. She needed to speak.

"This is a surprise," she said at length. "You picking me up," she added, mouth dry, voice low. "Because after the kiss they'd never spoken again."

"Alec is trapped in London and is hoping to sort it all out so he can come home for Christmas. Mr. Trimble, who does a lot of the driving for the family, has a touch of a bug, and is keeping away from everyone to keep others from coming down sick."

"And Cara? She'd said she'd get me."

He glanced at her as they crossed the parking lot. "She

hasn't told you?"

Ella frowned. "Told me what?"

"Nothing," he said, unlocking the trunk of his car and placing her luggage in it.

Ella wasn't deterred. Once in the car, she buckled her seatbelt and waited for Baird to get settled. "What's wrong with her?"

"Nothing's wrong. She's just…" His voice faded and he sighed. "You'll find out when you get there."

ELLA TOOK A slow breath, trying to calm herself. There was no reason she should feel so shaken. It was not as if she'd tumbled into bed with Baird at the wedding. They didn't get naked. There was nothing shameful about what happened. They'd kissed. Big deal. There shouldn't have been drama, either.

But after he'd walked away from her, he'd completely disappeared, and she'd looked for him now and then, confused, wondering how something so lovely had left her feeling so awful. As the evening came to an end, and she went to her hotel room, her heart felt battered, and her self-esteem was definitely bruised.

Why had she liked him? Why had she been so drawn to him? He wasn't as sophisticated as Cara's husband, nor was he dashing, but Baird was handsome in a rugged sort of way.

His features were that of a man who had been in a fight or two. His nose, had a strong bump in the bridge, making her think it had been broken more than once—which she found very sexy. She liked a man that looked like a man.

Baird was most definitely a man.

His features went with his very broad shoulders and his height and his long legs. His smile was crooked, and barely there, but it still made her insides do a little curl of pleasure. Whenever he was near her, she felt a little bit lightheaded and breathless. Ella wasn't sure if he felt the sparks, but she found him watching her, almost as often as she watched him.

BAIRD HAD MOST definitely not volunteered to pick up Ella Roberts from the Manchester airport.

He'd actually done everything possible to get out of the favor his best friend Alec Sherbourne had asked of him—short of offending Alec. Having been friends for twenty years now, Baird didn't mind doing favors for his best friend as Alec was quick to help him whenever Baird needed something. But chauffeuring beautiful Ella Roberts from one place to another wasn't something Baird could do. She'd proven to be seriously problematic in August and she wasn't good for his sanity.

When they'd been introduced at the wedding last August, there had been immediate sparks between them, an awareness he rarely felt with anyone. He hadn't been prepared for the intensity of the attraction, or the insistent desire, which only became stronger as the days passed. Baird didn't want or need temptation. His life was complicated at the moment, and he'd flown to the United States for Alec's wedding in need of some quiet and calm. But stunning Ella with her long red hair, sea blue eyes, and expressive face did not exert a calming influence on him.

If she'd been simply gorgeous, he could have dismissed her, but she was a brilliant scholar, one entering her final year of her PhD program with dozens of published papers already part of her resume.

Baird liked smart women. He loved smart, strong women. But he'd just come out of a long relationship, and he wasn't looking to start anything new. He certainly didn't need a one-stand affair with his best friend's young sister-in-law, a woman Alec was already calling his sister.

So no, Ella was not for him. She was as off limits as they came. Which is why he went to great lengths to avoid her. He'd never been rude. He knew better than that. Instead, he played the role of the charming, chivalrous guest from Scotland, kind to all, but cordially distant with Ella. He'd walk her down the aisle, pose for the requisite photos, check to see if she needed a drink before slipping away. That had been the goal—slip away. Move away. Stay away. And it had worked until Saturday night's reception when his discipline failed.

It would have been convenient to lay the blame on the glass of champagne he'd had for the toast, but he hadn't been drunk, not even buzzed.

It wasn't champagne, it wasn't the warm breezy evening with the moon reflecting off the water. It wasn't the music or the scent of roses and lilies. It was her, red curls spilling down her back, her lips curving, her smile tugging at his heart, making his body warm, making him crave a taste of the life that shone so brightly in her eyes. She was so expressive, so passionate, so alive. He wanted that, wanted her. His infamous control snapped, and taking her hand he drew her into the shadows down by the dock and kissed her as if his life depended on it. And for those few heady moments, it had.

Ella cleared her throat. "Do you know why my sister isn't the one picking me up?

Ella's question pulled Baird back to the present. "Why don't you ask her when you see her?" he asked, barely glancing in her direction. He would not be drawn back into her sphere. He was not going to be attracted to her again. August was months ago. He was a changed man.

Ella's laugh was mocking. "Do you not know the answer? Or do you just not want to tell me?"

"I just don't think it's my business to tell you."

"So, you do know."

He shrugged. "Alec is my best friend."

She sighed heavily, clearly exasperated by him. "Is she sick?"

"We'll be there in less than an hour."

"So, she's at least at Langley?"

"Yes."

"See? That wasn't so hard, Baird. I appreciate the straight answer."

His brow lifted. "Do your friends enjoy your sarcasm?"

"I think so."

He wanted to smile but he wouldn't let himself. "Hmm. I wouldn't be so sure."

"Do you even have friends?" she retorted a little too cheerfully. "Besides Alec, I mean?"

"I do, and I have a close family. We see each other often. Any other questions?"

"A few."

"Let's have them then, and once you're satisfied, perhaps we can just be silent."

Ella laughed. "You sound like an eighty-year-old man."

She made him feel like it, too. "So, what are your questions, Ella?"

"Do you have brothers or sisters? Or are you an only child?"

"Three sisters. I'm the only lad."

"And what a lad you are." Ella said before clearing her throat. "I was being sarcastic, too. That wasn't a compliment."

"Oh, I knew that," he assured her.

Silence followed. Ella had given up.

BAIRD DIDN'T SPEAK again until he began slowing down. "We're almost there," he said, pointing to the line of thick trees bordering the road. "That's all Langley Park. The house is set back on the property. You can't see it from the road. Those that rent the holiday cottages use this access road, but we'll go through the main gates."

Ella didn't know what she'd expected, but not all these open fields with the clusters of oak and sycamore trees. She wondered if the land was pastures or for crops. "Is this good farmland?" she asked.

"No. The Peak District lends itself more to sheep and cattle, and crops such as hay to feed the livestock. Some farmers have been successful with maize or some root crops, but it's not particularly arable. Most farms here are small."

"So, this isn't farmland?" she asked, pointing to the fields behind the stone wall.

"No. It's just what we call parkland."

Baird drove through huge gates and down a long driveway which gave quick views of an enormous red brick mansion, the center of the house flanked by two red brick wings of different heights and styles.

"Wow," Ella whispered.

"It never fails to impress me, too," Baird said. "The central house is Elizabethan and still has the original Tudor hall, but the exterior has been hidden by a Georgian façade."

The staff were gathering on the front steps as Baird parked the car. The older woman came down the stairs to greet Ella, introducing herself as Mrs. Booth the housekeeper, and sharing how pleased she was that Ella was here for Christmas and that her ladyship would be so happy to see her and she was in her room now, and if Ella was ready, she'd take her straight up to her sister.

"I am Mrs. Johnson, or Cook, as the earl calls me," the other woman said, coming forward to be introduced. "I make sure no one goes hungry here. Once you're settled with her ladyship, I will bring you a lunch tray. Your sister did not want to eat until you'd arrived."

Then before Ella could quite take in the grandeur of the house with its sweeping staircase that wrapped all three floors, or the glass dome topping the staircase, flooding the interior with light, Mrs. Booth was climbing the stairs pointing out things as she went. "This is the new part of the house," she said, "and this is the formal entrance when guests arrive. The main room the family gathers in is the green drawing room and that is the first room off the entry, with the music room adjacent."

They reached the second floor which was very high up due to the fourteen-foot ceilings. "To our right is the family wing, and to the left is the guest wing. Your sister shares the master bedroom with his lordship—"

"Is that strange?" Ella asked, rather amazed that Mrs. Booth could fly up the stairs and carry a conversation without being the least bit breathless.

Mrs. Booth stopped, expression thoughtful. "They are the first generation at Langley Park to share a bedroom, but they are a modern couple with a modern marriage." She began walking again, hustling them down the long hallway. "If there is anything you need, anything at all, just ask. We couldn't be happier to have you with us."

And then on reaching a closed door on the right, Mrs. Booth gave a firm knock and when Cara called, "Come in," she walked away.

Ella opened the door and peeked in, discovering it was a huge bedroom with an equally huge four-poster bed. The walls were papered in a rich blue, with luxurious velvet curtains of the same hue framing each of the tall windows. Cara looked like a doll in the big bed with the white sheets crumpled around her.

"What is going on?" Ella hurried to her sister's side and gave Cara a hug. "Everyone has me so worried."

"What have you been told?" Cara answered, hugging Ella back.

"Virtually nothing, but for you to be in bed, something must be wrong because you're always busy, always planning something." Ella drew back to examine her sister, but Cara didn't look sick. If anything, she appeared rosy. Happy.

"I'm so glad you're here," Cara said, pushing herself up higher and used an adjacent pillow to slip behind her back. "I've been counting down the days. I'm so bored and I want to hear everything … unless you're too tired?"

"Not too tired, but I do want to know what's happened to you. You haven't mentioned being unwell in any of our calls or texts."

"I'm not unwell, I just have to be careful."

"Careful of what?"

"I was going to wait until Alec was home, but he might not be home for a few days, so…" Cara smiled as she dragged out the suspense. "I'm pregnant."

"Cara!"

"With twins."

Ella sprang to her feet. "*Cara!*"

Cara laughed. "I know. I can hardly believe it myself. I thought Tom and Kristine had twins because of Kristine, but maybe it's our family? Who knows, but Alec and I haven't shared the news as there were some early complications, but now that I'm in week twenty they're resolving, and the risk of miscarriage is much less than it was. The doctor is still keeping me on bedrest, though, just to play it safe. I should be up and about in the new year."

"I'm glad your doctor is being cautious."

"We all are. Although I had hoped to be off bedrest by now. It's hard for me to not run around."

"Which is probably why your doctor is keeping you on bedrest through January." Ella laughed. "Twins, Cara. I can't believe it."

"I couldn't, either. We only found out I was pregnant

late September. I figured I was late due to the wedding and everything, but then I wasn't feeling well and bought a test. I was shocked. We were going to wait for a couple of years, but apparently God had a different plan. We had our first appointment with the obstetrician October ninth, and that's when the doctor said there were two heartbeats. I'm lucky I was already lying down. I think I would have fainted. I was beyond shocked. And Alec—his face! He was nervous about one baby, but two?" Cara grinned. "It's been quite an eventful few months. Certainly not the honeymoon phase we expected."

"You weren't on birth control?"

"Almost always using protection, but there was that time on the private island. The yacht had dropped us off and—"

"I got the picture. No intimate details necessary." But she was smiling so big. "But Alec's happy?"

"Very happy," Cara assured her. "He's been so protective of me. I could be up more, but he's insisting I stay in bed and take it easy. There's to be no stress, he says."

"So, you've cancelled your party this Saturday, then?"

Cara didn't immediately answer. "Alec wanted to," she confessed. "But I told him we need to have it. For his family. They've been waiting to celebrate us—our marriage—and they always come here for Christmas anyway."

"That doesn't mean you need to be throwing a party now, Cara. Wait until January. Wait until the babies are born. Then throw the party."

"Alex said the same thing, but the Sherbourne family is so looking forward to being together again, and the neighbors are excited as well. I don't want to let any of them down. I can be social. I just can't be on my feet for very long. Alec will carry me downstairs for the party and I'll sit in a comfortable chair and pretend I'm a queen and let everyone come to visit with me."

Ella no longer felt like smiling. Her sister could be so stubborn, and this was a perfect example of her refusing to be realistic. "I think this is a terrible idea. If Mom and Dad knew—"

"But they don't. I'm telling them on Christmas. It's my gift to them this year, especially as I haven't been able to do the shopping I would normally do."

"So, when is the baby—*babies*—due?"

"May thirteenth, but as you know from Tom and Kristine, twins often arrive early. My goal is to make it to week thirty-eight."

"So, who knows?"

"You're the first person I've told," Cara said. "Alec has told Baird, and the staff here knows, but that's it. We've promised them to secrecy, too. And they've been brilliant, waiting on me hand and foot, spoiling me rotten. Once Alec's home, we'll share the news with his family. I'd hoped he'd be back before they arrived but he's dealing with a lot at work and will only make it back Friday after work."

"When does his family arrive?"

"Friday, around noon."

"Friday, as in the day after tomorrow? The aunts and great uncle?" Ella saw Cara's nod and Ella felt a wave of indignation. "And they'll be here through Christmas, just like last year?"

Cara nodded a second time.

Ella jumped up and paced the elegant master bedroom. "How is Alec okay with this? You had to cater to them last year, do everything for them—"

"Only because the staff wasn't here, and then we had that huge storm. But the staff is staying on for the holidays this year. Mrs. Booth's adult children are coming here, they'll have rooms in the guest wing, and I've heard it's not going to be a white Christmas, which is too bad for you."

"Oh, Cara, I'm worried."

"Don't be. You met Mrs. Booth, our housekeeper and manager of all things important. If you haven't yet met Mrs. Johnson, the cook and keeper of the kitchen and all menu planning, you will. And then there's Mr. Trimble, our head groundskeeper, who also plays chauffeur, as you've already discovered. He's a lovely man, isn't he?"

"I haven't met Mr. Trimble."

"But he picked you up—"

"No, he didn't. Baird picked me up."

"Baird? Alec's Baird?"

"Yes," Ella answered flatly. "I wish someone had given me a head's up. I was caught off guard."

"I didn't know. Mr. Trimble was supposed to get you. That was the plan."

"Apparently, Mr. Trimble has the flu. He's been told to stay home and isolate so that he doesn't get anyone else here sick."

"Alec didn't tell me. I'm sorry." Cara leaned forward. "If I'd known, I would have made alternate arrangements for your arrival. I know how you feel about him." Cara searched Ella's eyes. "How was the drive home?"

"Fine." Ella hesitated, some of the anger fading. She returned to the bed and sat down again. "It's not as if I hate him. It's nothing like that. I'm just ... uncomfortable."

"I know." Cara reached for her hand, giving it a quick squeeze. "Believe me, if I'd known I would have booked a driver for you. I'll speak to Alec—"

"No, don't. Baird is his best friend, and it was really nice of him to take the time to get me. I don't imagine he would normally be in Manchester on a Wednesday."

"No, he'd be at his office in Edinburgh."

"Is that far from here?"

Cara wrinkled her nose. "About a five-hour drive. If there's no traffic."

Ella's heart sank. Baird had gone to a great deal of effort to pick her up. She would have to thank him—nicely—the next time she saw him. Hopefully, that wouldn't be anytime soon.

A knock sounded on the door and then it opened. Mrs.

Johnson entered with a tray and carried it to the foot of the bed. "It's an indoor picnic," she said, setting the tray down.

Ella suddenly felt very hungry and was so happy to see her favorite lunch, grilled cheese and apple slices. There were also two glasses of milk and slices of a fragrant spice cake that had to be right out of the oven.

Ella eased off her shoes and sat cross-legged on the bed, happily eating while asking Cara questions about everything from when was dinner usually served, and were the holiday tours still taking place at Langley because Ella hadn't noticed any crowds or cars when she'd arrived today.

"Alec had them end early," Cara said. "He didn't want a lot of people in and out of the house when I was alone here. Well, not alone, as you can see, but without him."

"Were you glad?"

"I was. It's a lot of noise and a lot of cars parking and coming and going. I think next year I might stay in London with Alec and the babies until the tours are over."

"Or maybe the tours can just take place on weekends, instead of every day from November until Christmas?"

Cara nodded thoughtfully "That's a good suggestion, and it used to be that way. Maybe with young children we'll try that next year and see how it goes. It's not as if we can't try and see what works best for us as a family."

"I agree." Ella gathered all their empty dishes, stacking them on the tray. "I'm going to take this downstairs with me and let you rest."

Cara smothered a yawn. "I am getting sleepy."

"Then sleep, and I'll be back for dinner. Do I come back upstairs?"

"If you don't mind."

"I don't mind." Ella gave her sister one last quick hug before taking the tray downstairs with her.

Mrs. Booth must have been waiting for her as she came forward immediately and relieved Ella of the tray. "Let me take this to the kitchen and then I can drive you to the cottage. If you're ready. Usually, Mr. Trimble would be here to drive you, but with him gone, we're all filling in."

"I'd be happy to walk," Ella said. "The more I move, the better I'll sleep tonight."

"In that case, I will have one of the boys run your luggage down to you. I promise you'll have them soon."

"If you're sure that won't put anyone out?"

"Not at all," Mrs. Booth assured her before giving Ella walking directions for the cottage.

Chapter Two

With the walking directions fresh in her mind, Ella thanked the housekeeper and stepped out through the back door of the massive red brick house and into the late afternoon sunshine. The sun wasn't very warm, but at least it wasn't raining. The next few days were forecast to be cool but dry, which was a nice change since Bellingham had been raining when Ella left home yesterday.

She passed a series of buildings, one with a sign that read Tickets in the bottom window, and an area in the distance with chains, which must have been the tour parking lot.

She walked on and after a few minutes a two-story stone cottage came into view, the second floor marked by four windows, with four more on the ground floor. A fresh green wreath with a dark red ribbon hung on the front door. The front door was open and a small fire glowed in the hearth. The interior of the cottage was stone, the ceiling covered in dark beams. Sturdy bookshelves flanked the stone fireplace with comfortable furniture grouped before the impressive hearth. She lightly ran a hand across the back of the soft caramel brown, leather couch before taking a seat in one of the dark blue upholstered chairs by the fireplace. The chair was just perfect, the back slightly rounded, the cushion welcoming. She had a feeling she'd spend a lot of time in this chair, reading, relaxing, and just dreaming about a future where she was done with school because no one knew how much she was struggling with the career choice she'd made and the hours—and money—invested in her studies.

She was still sitting by the impressive hearth, studying the old stone, when the door opened and Baird entered carrying her two pieces of luggage.

"I was asked to bring these here," he said placing them on the floor. "I didn't ask why but should have. I think they've sent you to the wrong cottage."

"But this is my cottage. Cara just confirmed it less than a half hour ago."

"That's not what Alec told me. He personally made arrangements for me to stay here, in this cottage, so I can work without being in the family's way." Baird gave her a significant look. "Not to be unkind, but I think he was including you in the family."

"I'm sorry, but you and Alec have it wrong. Ever since August when Cara invited me to come for Christmas, I've been promised the cottage, *this* cottage, the one she stayed in while she was here last year. Alec may have forgotten the arrangements, but Cara certainly hasn't, and Mrs. Booth knew as well as she was the one who gave me walking directions here."

"Perhaps she meant the dairy."

"Perhaps you're the one meant to be in the dairy," Ella flashed. "If you're so concerned, you can run up to the house and ask where you belong."

Baird crossed his arms. "I'm not about to return to the house and make a scene."

"Neither am I." She matched his pose, arms folded every bit as defiantly.

"Since it appears that Alec and Cara are having communication issues, I think its best if we sort this out ourselves, without needing to drag them in to this. We aren't children, after all."

"No indeed," she said stiffly, "and since you need a place to work, I'd suggest Alec's study would be ideal for you. Or perhaps the library at the house? Both must be available."

"Until Alec returns," Baird answered, "and I'm not going to move my things twice. I'm settled here already. I'm staying here. You're not unpacked. You haven't moved in—" He broke off at the firm knock on the front door.

Ella swept past him to open the door, revealing a young man in a heavy coat on the doorstep with a basket of glass bottles, jars, jams and baked goods.

"From Mrs. Johnson," the young man said. "She thought you might need something for tea later and said to just let her know if you need anything else to be comfortable."

Ella couldn't resist throwing a victorious look in Baird's direction even as she took the basket from the young man.

"Please give Mrs. Johnson my sincere thanks," she said, smiling warmly.

He nodded, closed the door behind him and Ella placed the oversized basket on the rustic dining room table. "You were saying?" she asked Baird sweetly.

He wasn't smiling, and his expression was anything but sweet. "You aren't settled in yet, and your sister is in the house. Shouldn't you be with her? Doesn't it make you feel a tad bit guilty that she's all alone in the house and you're avoiding her here—"

"Not avoiding her, Mr. MacLauren, and the rooms in the family wing have all been assigned from what I understand. Cara is happy I'm here and so am I." Ella's chin rose. "And while you might think you're entitled to the cottage because you have work to do, I think being British, or Welsh, or whatever you are—"

"Scottish," he ground out.

She waved a hand carelessly, deliberately being obtuse just to get under his skin. "Kind of all the same to me," she said, suppressing a laugh because of course they weren't the same, but she wasn't feeling nice, not after all the heartache he'd given her. "The point is you live in the UK. You can come see Alec any time. You do not need to be in the cottage, not this Christmas. Since I'm the guest, you can be a gentleman and clear out."

"No."

"No? Are we to act like children instead, requiring Alec

and Cara to settle this for us?"

"Again no." Baird's voice sounded low and hard. "We settle this ourselves. There's no need to draw them into our drama."

"It shouldn't be a drama." Ella pulled a chair out at the table and sat down. "I'm twenty-five and you're what? Forty?"

"Nearly thirty-five." Baird's jaw tightened, jutting, his light golden-brown eyes narrowing. "You can't still be upset about August. I've apologized."

Her mouth fell open, and she had to force herself to snap it closed. He apologized for kissing her, which she didn't ask for, or didn't need. She'd enjoyed the kiss and then he'd ruined it with his apology.

"August?" Ella frowned, acting confused. "What happened?" She pretended to continue thinking hard. She shook her head. "I don't remember."

"So, you're not just being difficult because I kissed you," he said walking toward her and yanking out a chair at the table. "Because I'd be happy to apologize again if it means—"

"That I leave?" She laughed. "No. Sorry, Charlie, I'm staying. And whatever you think I'm upset about has nothing to do with me being here in the cottage, excited to have a little place of my own for the next two weeks. I share a house in Bellingham with two other grad students. I never have space, or quiet, and you have no idea how much I've looked forward to having a little bit of me time."

"The main house is huge. You could have an entire wing to yourself. Plenty of me time." He paused for effect. "You also have the very unique opportunity to experience Christmas in a great English country house."

"It is a grand house," she agreed, surprised by how much she was enjoying herself. She rarely debated anyone who wasn't an undergraduate student. "Maybe you were raised with lots of staff, but its more comfortable here, having access to my own kitchen, not worrying that I'm in the way, or putting anyone out."

"I was raised in a very middle-class family. We had no help. But you're not putting the Langley Park staff out. It's Mrs. Booth and Mrs. Johnson's job to take care of you."

"That is my whole point. I don't want them to take care of me, not when Cara needs so much support right now, and with Alec's family arriving Friday, and all three elderly, there is no need for me to be underfoot." She shrugged delicately, pleased when his grim expression darkened further. He really wasn't happy. Good. His glowering and growling made her happy.

"Let's be honest," she said lightly, invigorated, and closing strong, "the last thing anyone needs is an American houseguest with jet lag waking up in the middle of the night, wandering through corridors trying to find the kitchen for a snack. That's asking for trouble, whether it's me falling down the stairs breaking my neck, or crashing into one of those medieval armor suits on the landing, and breaking my neck—"

"That would only happen if you take the staircase in the old part of the house," he interrupted curtly. "Use the new staircase. Safer for all."

"Oh, the one from the early nineteenth century, not the fourteenth century? Much, much newer, yes."

He turned away and ran a hand over his face and she thought he was about to shout or throw something, but when he looked at her a moment later, his lips twitched, amusement glinting in his eyes. "You're impossible."

For a moment, she wasn't charmed. She refused to be charmed. Even by that lovely accent of his, and then she smiled, a very small smile, but he saw it.

"I'm simply trying to protect Alec from an accident waiting to happen." Ella smoothed her hair back from her face thinking that when she last looked in the mirror she looked like a hedgehog, but it couldn't be helped. "I imagine he has great homeowners' insurance—you'd have to with a home that size—but there's far less danger here in the cottage, to myself and the Sherbourne family antiquities." She hesitated. "You aren't his lawyer, by chance, are you?"

"No. Thank heavens."

"You're not corporate law?"

"I used to practice corporate law, but now I specialize in family law."

"What is that here?' she asked, thinking she should know it.

"Divorces. Child custody cases."

Ella wrinkled her nose in distaste. "I would hate that."

"I do."

"Then why work in that area of law?"

"I'm good at it." He shrugged. "And it pays well."

"I would have thought corporate law paid better."

"Generally speaking, yes, but I was spending more time in New York and Hong Kong than I was in the UK, and that grew old quickly." His brow creased and he glanced toward the small kitchen off the entry. "Did you want a cup of tea?"

"Are you offering to make me a cup of tea in my kitchen?" she asked innocently.

"I moved in yesterday," he reminded her. "My kitchen. But since this cottage means so much to you, you can stay. I won't kick you out. There are four bedrooms upstairs. You are welcome to any of them, except the one I've taken."

"I'd like to kick you out. I'm trying very hard to remove you from the premises."

He flashed a grin, teeth white, and his sheer magnetism hit her all over again. "I know," he said sympathetically, "but it won't happen. You might be stubborn, but I'm more stubborn than you. I've been accused of being a rock. Immoveable. And since I'm unpacked, settled, and happy here, I'm staying." He stood in the middle of the kitchen and gave her a quizzical look. "Tea?"

"Please."

He smiled, a smile that did crazy things to her insides.

She looked away, horrified he was doing it again, already. Making her feel warm and tingly. Making her pulse race. Making her yearn for more in the most ridiculous way.

But this time would be different.

This time she would not fall for his charm. She didn't have to be cold and harsh, but she certainly couldn't let down her guard, couldn't go soft. "Are you absolutely certain you don't want the guest wing? It's really special."

"Ah, yes, the original one, with unreliable plumbing and heating, and the Sherbourne ghost. Fortunately, I'm happy here. My bed is comfortable. The water takes a bit to heat, but the fireplace keeps things toasty downstairs. Best of all, no ghostly apparitions, either."

"None at all?" Ella asked, glancing up at the narrow staircase that led to the second floor.

"I haven't experienced any, but who knows what might happen in your room. Your English adventure awaits."

"I suppose I should get settled." Ella picked up her luggage and carried it carefully up the steep narrow staircase, quite sure that it wasn't up to any modern building code. She opened the first door she came to, and it faced the woods, and the light was already gone, leaving the room in shadows.

She opened the next door, and this was much brighter, and it faced the main house. It wasn't large, but the dark beams and square windows set in thick stone walls felt cozy. A thick comforter covered the bed, the linens a dusty rose with dark green embroidery. The bed's pillow shams were also pink and green while the curtains framing the windows were dark green. The only chair in the room was upholstered in a soft pink chintz fabric. A small pretty landscape on the wall featured a little girl in a white dress and bonnet, her arms wrapped around the neck of a red spaniel. The room was charming but feminine. No wonder Baird chose the other room.

Ella went back downstairs for hot tea, and Baird poured her a cup from the teapot on the counter. A small plate of homemade scones and butter and jam were to be shared.

"Thank you," she said, taking a sip of tea and then unable to swallow as she felt just how close Baird was. They were practically elbow to elbow due to the kitchen being so small and it felt just a little too intimate for her. "I might sneak back upstairs and take a bath."

"Remember it takes time for the water to warm. Wait to undress until the tub is half full, otherwise you could freeze to death. I learned the hard way yesterday."

She pictured him standing naked impatiently waiting for the water to warm, and the picture in her head made her blush. "I'll keep that in mind," she said, face hot. "Oh, and if you don't see me up by six, could you please wake me? I'm supposed to join Cara for dinner."

"Will do."

WHILE ELLA SLEPT, Baird worked at the table, reading through his client's wife's testimony. She was demanding full custody and financial support for her and both children, equal to what she'd enjoyed during their marriage. She claimed her husband was cold and abusive, stating he had little involvement in their children's lives, and when he was present, he was frequently cruel and always critical.

His client claimed he'd been a victim from the start. His wife was a master manipulator and had tricked him into marrying her, convincing him she was pregnant with his child. It wasn't until the baby arrived early, and looked nothing like him, that he suspected he'd been played. When he paid for a secret DNA test, the results were exactly as he suspected. He wasn't the father, and when she announced she was pregnant again, he didn't care. He wanted nothing to do with her or the children.

Baird flipped through the next few pages of testimony before closing it and pushing the paperwork away. None of the testimony surprised him. Nothing anyone did surprised him anymore. Thank goodness he wasn't a judge, and he didn't need to make the ruling. He just had to represent his client in court and let the system do the rest.

His phone vibrated on the table. It was Alec calling. Finally.

Baird took his phone, grabbed his coat, and stepped outside. He'd been waiting for Alec to call him all day.

Closing the cottage door behind him, Baird stiffened at

the cold. It had grown dark in the past two hours, night coming early now that they were so close to the winter solstice. Tucking the phone between his jaw and shoulder, he snapped the buttons on his coat, a vintage jacket his dad had owned and passed on to him when it no longer fit him. "How are you, Alec?"

"Still trying to figure out just how much has gone missing. The loss is staggering."

"Has anyone found Phelps?"

"No. The police don't think he's left the country. His wife Helen believes he's at a business conference and will be home for Christmas."

"Has no one told her the truth?"

"I haven't. I have to speak to all our clients first." Alec sighed. "But he's the last one I would have ever suspected to embezzle client funds. James was my father's protégé. Langley Investments' second in command. Dad trusted James more than anyone. More than me."

Baird knew all about that. Alec's dad had always been incredibly hard on him. "What about the City Police? What are they doing?"

"They're looking for Phelps, and Scotland Yard is following up on some leads, but he isn't using his phone anymore, not since I contacted him. I should have waited. I should have brought in the detectives before calling him."

"But as you said yesterday, it never crossed your mind that James was at the heart of this. Of course, you turned to him. He was your right hand. He had access to all accounts." Baird hesitated. "When do you think the news will go public?"

"Soon, which is why I'm calling all clients in the morning, letting them know what's happened, and assuring them their accounts are safe, and they will get everything back."

"Can you do that?"

"It won't be easy, but I won't let any of our clients suffer because I wasn't paying attention."

"You're not responsible."

"But I am." Alec was silent a moment. "How is everything there? Is Ella settling in okay?"

"Yes." Baird realized he'd need to wake her soon. "She's happy to be here and she's having dinner with Cara tonight. Speaking of Cara, when are you going to tell her what's happened?"

"I don't want to upset her. She doesn't need the stress."

"But it will be more upsetting for her to hear about it on the evening news, when everyone else does."

"I know. Just hoping we can get through Christmas before the news breaks. That would truly be a Christmas miracle."

Baird felt for Alec. "Don't worry about us, or anything here. Do what you have to do there. I've everything under control here. Well, at least until your aunts and Uncle Frederick arrive. Then it's game over."

Alec's laugh was raw. "They're not that bad," he protested. Then after a moment, added, "Well, maybe they are, but in a good way. They'll keep you busy. Ella just needs to plan lots of games and activities. That's what Cara did last year, and it worked like a charm."

"We'll do our best."

"Thank you, Baird."

"Glad I can be here."

Back inside, Baird crossed to the fire blazing in the hearth, standing before it to chase away the chill. But the chill wasn't just from the night. He was concerned for Alec, and worried about Cara who had no idea why her husband was still in London, fighting to save the family firm. Unlike in the United States where companies had limited liability should the company fail to pay its debts, there was no such protection in the United Kingdom meaning business owners had unlimited personal liability when a company failed. Which was why Alec was scrambling to save what he could.

ELLA WAS WOKEN to a brisk knock on the door. She opened her eyes, but her head ached.

Another knock sounded on the door. "Ella, it's six. You asked me to wake you up so you could meet Cara for dinner."

Yawning, Ella dragged herself into a sitting position. "Yes, thank you."

"I can drive you up when you're ready," he replied.

Baird's footsteps retreated, but she couldn't make herself move for a second. She'd been sleeping deeply, and her brain was groggy. Finally, she forced herself out of bed, into the hall to the shared bathroom. Pulling her long hair back with a scrunchie she splashed cold water on her face. The cold water wasn't merely cold, it was frigid, and she gasped but it did the trick. She was waking up.

Five minutes later, Ella was downstairs dressed in jeans and a pretty sweater with soft sheepskin lined ankle boots on to keep her feet warm. The boots had been her splurge before the trip, but as she and Baird stepped outside into the clear cold night, she was glad she'd bought them.

"I think I'd like to walk up to the house," she said, glancing at Baird. "I'd like to move a bit and I know the way. I can see the lights from here."

"I'll walk with you then."

"You don't have to."

His eyebrow lifted. "I know. But I'd enjoy the walk, too. Might help me clear my head."

Interesting he'd say that. She'd thought he seemed troubled as she joined him at the foot of the stairs.

"Something happen?" she asked, wrapping her scarf more snugly around her throat as they set off.

"Just business. But it'll get sorted. It's tough when there are problems this time of year."

She glanced at his profile. "Problems are never fun, especially not days before Christmas. Hopefully, it won't ruin your holidays."

The corner of his mouth quirked but the smile didn't reach his eyes. "Hopefully not."

They walked the rest of the way in silence, with the quiet suddenly broken by barking dogs, and then the labs came rushing to meet them, two of them sprinting, with the oldest hanging back, staying close to the light shining next to the mudroom door.

Mrs. Booth had left for the night, but Mrs. Johnson was there in the kitchen, and she told Ella to go on up to Cara's room as dinner was ready and she'd be up shortly with their meal.

Ella glanced at Baird as he pulled out a kitchen stool and sat down. "You're not joining us?"

"No. Have your sister time. Mrs. Johnson and I have a football match to watch."

But it was Baird who appeared at the master bedroom door with a huge tray filled with covered dishes. He carried the tray to the bench at the foot of the huge four-poster bed. "I promised Mrs. Johnson I'd serve you," he said, lifting the silver domed lids revealing fragrant roast chicken, golden brown roasted potatoes and colorful root vegetables.

"No, no we can manage," Cara said, shooing him away. "We don't need a manservant, even one as handsome as you."

Baird's smiled, amused. "Handsome, am I?"

Ella rolled her eyes. "Cara said it, not me."

He just laughed and exited the room.

As the door closed Cara turned to her. "What did happen between you? You never said."

Ella focused on organizing her sister's dinner, picking up a linen napkin and the necessary cutlery. "Nothing important. We just ... didn't get along."

"And yet, that's not my impression, seeing you two together." Cara smoothed her covers over her lap. "You two are rather sparky—"

"Not so."

"I'd go so far as to say there's a definite *thing*."

"You mean, *nothing*." Ella glanced around looking for a proper bed tray for Cara's dinner. "What do you usually eat on?"

"I just balance on my lap."

"But what if it's hot? Or it spills?" Ella emptied the big tray, placed it across Cara's lap and then put her dinner plate on the tray. "That's better."

"Thank you," Cara said. "Now, as we were discussing Baird—"

"But we weren't." Ella sat down in a chair near Cara, balancing her own plate on her knee. "And we shouldn't. I know he's Alec's best friend, but he and I didn't get along at the wedding. We just rubbed each other the wrong way."

"Mrs. Booth made it sound like you're sharing the cottage with him." Cara's blue eyes were wide, her expression ingenuous. "Did I misunderstand her?"

"No."

"Isn't that going to be problematic considering you *rub* each other the wrong way?"

Ella heard how her sister emphasized the word rub and wondered if Cara knew what happened between Ella and Baird at the reception, but if that was true, why wouldn't Cara have mentioned it before? Cara had never been able to keep that a secret. Ella might not have a poker face, but Cara could be counted on blurting things, particularly juicy things.

Ella took a bite of the roasted potatoes and chewed. They were delicious. Melt in your mouth delicious. "This is what happened, and there's really no problem. You promised me the cottage. Alec promised Baird the cottage. Baird refused to move out, and I wasn't going to give in. I've been excited about staying there since you invited me after the wedding. If Baird is miserable, he can stay in the guest wing here."

Cara just smiled. "So, what bedroom did you choose?"

"The second one that faces the house. The green and pink room."

"And Baird?"

"The bedroom at the end, that faces the same view. But I don't know what his room looks like, I haven't seen it." Ella stabbed another crispy potato. "I need you to tell me the truth."

"Always."

"Were you hoping I would stay here, in the house, with you? Baird said that Alec said I was supposed to. If you want me here, I'll come back tonight. I just never got that impression—"

"Because you're supposed to be in the cottage. And when Aunt Emma and Aunt Dorothy arrive on Friday, they'll be here on this floor, and it's fine for them to share the bath, but I don't think it would be comfortable for the three of you to share. There was another one but we're shifting things around, trying to make room for the new elevator and so we don't have the space, and facilities, we normally do. Hopefully by next Christmas, the elevator will work."

"And the third bathroom?"

"Will be carved from one of the old dressing rooms." Cara cut her chicken breast into small bites. "I am anxious for Alec to return, though. He was supposed to come home last weekend—he always returns on weekends—but he couldn't, not with work. I haven't seen him since the tenth, which is so long for us."

"And you don't want to be in London with him?"

"It's better to be at Langley Park. I enjoy London when I can walk and shop and explore, but stuck in bed? No, this is more comfortable, especially with the dogs."

Ella set her plate on the nightstand. "Are you really going through with this party? It seems so stressful just before Christmas."

"The staff are doing so much of the work. Mrs. Booth

and Mrs. Johnson have the cleaning and prep in hand. The aunts' bedrooms are ready. They share a suite just down the hall. Uncle Frederick's suite is on the ground floor off the mudroom. The mudroom is probably the door you use when you leave the house to go to the cottage, and then when you return. It's where everyone hangs their coats and rubber boots, the dog leashes and more.

"I am familiar with it."

"I tried to order a few gifts online, but they haven't arrived yet and might not come now until January. If the gifts aren't here by late Friday, would you be willing to do some shopping for me on Saturday?"

"Before the party?"

"It would just mean popping into Bakewell. You could walk there and then take a cab home, or even arrange to have packages picked up. Everyone in town knows Langley Park. Shops would be happy to deliver packages if need be."

"They won't know me, though."

"They'll know you're my American sister. There won't be any problem." Cara chewed her lip, suddenly pensive. "Did Baird mention anything about Alec's work?"

"Only that he's trying to wrap things up so he can come home."

"That's what Alec tells me, too."

"Do you not believe him?"

Cara sighed, troubled. "I'm not sure. Something feels off. I just don't know what it is."

Bundled up, Ella walked briskly back to the cottage, the night cold and crisp, making her cheeks sting. Opening the door to the cottage, she discovered Baird in a chair near the fire reading and making notes. He was wearing a black wool cardigan and wearing dark glasses and with his square jaw and thick brown hair he reminded her of a sexy Scottish Clark Kent.

"Hello," Cara greeted, sliding off her coat and hanging it by the front door.

Baird glanced up and closed his book. "How is she?"

"Good." Ella approached the fire, tugging off her gloves. "She mostly talked about Alec's family arriving and Saturday's party. She also mentioned I might need to do some shopping for her if gifts don't arrive by Friday." Ella dropped into the chair opposite his. "I don't mind a to-do list, but I do mind that she's trying to oversee a party from her bedroom. Where is Alec? Why isn't he here? If he wants the party, he should be here managing everything, not leaving it to his bedridden wife."

"I don't think he wants the party." Baird pulled his glasses off and rubbed the bridge of his nose. "But he knows she's looked forward to the holidays for ages and doesn't want to disappoint her."

"I think him not being here is what's disappointing her."

"Did she say that?"

"Not in those exact words, but shouldn't he be here? What is keeping him in London? How is work so important that he can't return to his pregnant wife who's trapped in bed and expecting a house full of elderly people on Friday."

"It's not exactly a houseful. There are three relatives arriving, the two aunts and Alec's great uncle Frederick, but I agree that hosting a party isn't the best plan right now. They can always have the party later."

"Yes, later. After the babies arrive. Have you talked to Alec about it?"

"He and I have talked, and he's dealing with a lot at the moment, so he's leaving the decision to Cara. He knows she's isolated here, and she wants to make friends, and get to know the neighbors. In her mind, this is her chance to make friends."

"Alec does not strike me as a party person," Ella said.

"He's not."

Ella fell silent as she watched the fire burn, the crackle and pop satisfying in a way she couldn't explain. "Are Alec and Cara doing okay?" She glanced up, her gaze locking with Baird's. "They're not having any marital issues, are they?"

"Not that I've heard, but Alec isn't the type to overshare. He's British. The infamous stiff upper lip and all."

"Scottish people aren't like that?"

"We Scots like to gab more and drink more. Or so they say."

"Have you told Alec he just needs to put his foot down?

Because once he does, that's it. Cara wouldn't go against him. She's too madly in love with him to upset him."

"He feels the same about her, which is why he hasn't put his foot down, not that Alec would ever do that. He's a modern man, none of that Neanderthal behavior from him." Baird's voice dropped, a silkiness in his tone that sent a shiver through her, reminding her of how intensely he'd made her feel last summer.

It had been instant chemistry ... at least on her part.

"Unlike me."

Another tiny tremor raced through her. "I wouldn't call you a Neanderthal."

"No?"

"You're more civilized than that, more cultured. You have a lot of Celt in you." She thought for a moment. "I know the Vikings were raiders and warlike, but Celts were, too, from what I remember."

"Do I strike you as warlike?"

She studied him and then nodded. "But it's okay. I can handle you."

His gaze met hers and held, the air around them suddenly taut, electric. This was exactly what happened in August. This same heat, this same intensity. It took everything in her to turn away when her heart was racing and her head felt dizzy. "Seems like a good time to call it a night," she said huskily, before climbing the stairs to her room.

Chapter Three

Upstairs in her room, Ella leaned against the door, pulse still thudding, desire still flooding her.

For months, she'd managed to suppress the memory of how strongly she'd reacted to him when they met in August.

She'd forgotten how intense her response to him had been. But now, face-to-face with the desire, the memories came flooding back. Meeting him had turned her inside out. Within minutes—seconds—of meeting Baird, Ella felt undone.

She was no longer the disciplined grad student who kept her classes enthralled with her passion for literature, and the women who wrote those books. She had dissolved into a breathless, hapless, painfully self-conscious creature, exactly the kind of women Ella despised because women were meant to be strong, and self-sufficient. Women were meant to lead and inspire, not melt around men. But Baird was not your run of the mill man. He wasn't American, or comfortable, or endearingly familiar. He was a cross between Gerard Butler, a young Russell Crowe, with a hefty measure of *Outlander* star, Sam Heughan, thrown in. In short, Baird was perfect.

His effect on her was immediate and telling, and she didn't know if it was because he was tall—easily six-three—and muscular, like a rugby player. Or if it was because he was articulate and confident, a man who'd attended the best schools in Britain and was rumored to be a ruthless attorney with more clients and cases than time.

Ella was not as worldly. A brainy book girl from Bellingham, Washington, she'd always loved books by female writers, stories popular amongst women. She didn't really care if men read her favorite authors. She didn't care if her favorite authors' books were heavy on marriage, and family. She liked that they featured happy endings, liked that romance had happy endings. She liked them so much she chose to study them as an undergrad and then as her PhD.

But Baird ... Baird knocked her out of her cozy female realm into unfamiliar territory. She'd dated, she'd had boyfriends, but none of them were men like Baird.

The first night at the Friday Harbor resort had been just family and the wedding party—Cara, Alec, Ella the bridesmaid, and Alec's best man, Baird MacLauren.

Cara had mentioned Baird to Ella, saying he lived and worked in Edinburgh, and was an attorney. Cara failed to mention Baird was gorgeous and had the sexiest accent. Ella tried to play it cool the first few days, unwilling to smile too much in his direction, not wanting him to think she was flirting with him, and it seemed to work. They successfully avoided each other Thursday, too.

But Friday was the rehearsal and then the rehearsal dinner, two things they would be together for, and Ella pretended to be oblivious of Baird as more guests arrived and Alec introduced Baird to others. But when she looked for him at one point, she discovered he was watching her. She didn't look away, either. She couldn't. Something silent passed between them, a moment she couldn't articulate, but it was real and intense and unnerving.

That was the beginning, and the awareness only grew, heat and sparks flaring, the energy palpable. They barely interacted until the wedding rehearsal, and it wasn't until the wedding planner instructed them to face each other in the chapel and then meet in the middle of the aisle where Ella was to take his arm and they'd walk out together right behind the bride and groom.

"Closer, sister of the bride," the harried event planner called out. "And smile. This is a joyous occasion, not a funeral."

Everyone laughed but Ella didn't. Baird didn't, either. Instead, he tucked her hand more firmly in the crook of his arm. "I won't bite you, lass," he said quietly.

"I didn't think you would," she answered unsteadily, hoping he couldn't tell how hard her heart was pounding. She didn't know why he did this to her. She didn't understand this connection.

"Then why so shy?" he asked as they exited the chapel into the late afternoon sunlight.

She looked up into his face and their eyes met, the sun reflecting in his irises. His eyes weren't just light brown, they were brown with bits of gold and silver, but mostly gold, and Ella couldn't look away. She felt lost, alien to herself.

"I should go help Cara," she said, slipping her hand from his arm. "I'm sure I'll see you later."

She practically ran from him, desperate to escape, but as she hid in her hotel room trying to gather herself, she couldn't shake the sensation that she was burning. His touch, just his hand on hers had made her tingle, and pleasure still hummed in her. What on earth was happening?

Dinner that evening was even more problematic. She and Baird had been seated together at the same table, and the table was small and crowded, and Baird was close to her side. His shoulder periodically brushed hers, his thigh frequently touched hers, his body emanating heat that seeped into her.

All evening she tried to avoid looking into his eyes because they scorched her. She sat feeling naked, exposed, yearning for things that Ella Roberts did not yearn for. Ella Roberts did not yearn, and yet…

The tension ratchetted up all evening, and it was a relief to just go to bed. The wedding was the next day, and by the time she walked out of the chapel on Baird's arm, she was just so glad the wedding was over. She wanted the tension gone. She wanted to know how he kissed and if the kiss would deliver on the promise of the heat sizzling between them. She needed to kiss him to know. She almost hoped she'd be disappointed by the kiss, that in his arms she felt nothing. That his mouth on hers just left her cold.

During the reception, they had to dance together, and when Baird took her in his arms and drew her against him, she shuddered and he felt it, his eyes locking with hers, her body tingling from head to toe. When his hand settled in the small of her back she could barely breathe. Her body knew him. Her body recognized something in him, and she felt as if she was falling, falling into him. They moved on the dance floor, the music all around them, but she heard nothing, saw nothing but Baird.

Light gold eyes, dark thick hair, striking cheekbones and that firm mouth, a mouth she wanted to kiss.

The dance ended and conversation swirled around her, but she couldn't focus on it, not when Baird remained at her side, his hand light on her back, his fingertips warm, stirring something deep inside of her, making her hot, making her his.

Her parents came over and they were talking about the beautiful night and cake and wasn't everything so wonderful?

She nodded and said something appropriate. Then Baird said something appropriate. Her parents moved on, and the next second Baird took her hand and led her from the ballroom. They walked outside into the night, the white moon full, stars brilliant overhead. They passed guests, they turned a corner, and then another, walking down toward the water, and there, at the boathouse, his mouth found hers and it was everything she'd hoped and feared, everything she needed. Craved.

Him. She craved him.

Her arms slid around his neck, her fingers slipping into the cool thick strands of hair at his nape, and she answered his kiss as if a woman drowning. And maybe she was. She felt pushed to the edge of reason.

His kiss was everything. His kiss made her want a future with him, a future where she could always feel this real and alive, this sensitive and physical. In his arms, she wasn't just a brain, wasn't a girl with intelligent thoughts, but a flesh and blood woman made of skin and nerves, heart and hope.

The chilly cottage bedroom forced Ella to action. Shivering, she pushed away from the door and stripped off her clothes before tugging on pajamas. Her pajamas felt icy which cooled her heated skin. Her bed was cold, too, and she curled up in the stiff chilly sheets, cold from the bed, even as she was remembering August again and how the hot, dizzying kiss always ended the same.

With him breaking away from her, with him saying, *This should not have happened. It was a mistake.* He was not free.

How that hurt. Remembering now, months later, still hurt.

It would have been better to have never kissed him, better not to know how good his mouth felt, how good he felt then to experience pleasure only to be rejected.

It was why she hadn't wanted to see him again. He

wasn't a bad person. She didn't hate him. She could forgive him for the fierce hungry kiss. She could forgive him for making her body feel so beautiful. But she couldn't forgive him for what he'd done to her heart.

Maybe that wasn't right of her. Maybe she shouldn't hold it against him, but she'd kissed plenty of men and no one had ever threatened her sense of self, no one had touched her heart. Her heart wasn't easily captured, either.

No, Ella wasn't one to fall in love. But Baird's kiss had almost done it. His kiss had almost done her in.

BAIRD DIDN'T SLEEP well, waking repeatedly only to tell himself to stop thinking and just sleep.

It wasn't easy to stop thinking when Ella was just down the narrow hall. He hadn't expected to be sharing the cottage with her. He'd been certain she'd be in the house close to her sister. A wise man would move out of the cottage immediately, but Baird did not want to be in the house. He'd visited Langley Park before and was always overwhelmed by the sheer size of it, and the number of staff, and the grandeur of the interior. He'd grown up in a firmly middle-class family in Glasgow, as the youngest of four and the only son.

After three daughters his parents were thrilled to have a boy and Baird never lacked for anything. His older sisters used to tease him that he was spoiled rotten, but even they doted on him. Yes, he was spoiled rotten—he knew every day how much he was loved. He never took their love for granted, and he never asked for things he knew his parents couldn't afford.

He wasn't supposed to go to Eton. His family didn't send the girls to expensive private schools, never mind boarding school. Baird was happy in the local school, but his teachers immediately recognized Baird's potential. For years, they spoke of Baird's undeniable intellectual gifts. He needed more than what they could offer him. He would flourish with a challenging curriculum. Baird's family explored options, but they were all so incredibly expensive.

When he was twelve, his headmaster mentioned the King's Scholarship at Eton, sharing that it was an incredibly demanding exam, but if needed, the award could cover everything—tuition, fees, room and board. The headmaster believed Baird should try. Only fourteen scholarships were awarded every year, but if Baird studied and prepared, who knew?

The last thing Baird wanted was to go away for school. He was happy with his family, happy with his sports, and his older sisters who continued to spoil him rotten. But to appease his parents, who were truly good parents, he studied for the exam, taking it the next May when he was thirteen.

It was an incredibly difficult exam, an exhausting exam that left Baird feeling empty. He was certain he hadn't done well. He knew some things, but some of the papers and subjects were beyond him. He did what he could, the best he could, and no one was more surprised than him when he won one of the coveted King's Scholarships for September.

He did not want to go but his parents were so proud—their son, their Baird, their baby—had succeeded in earning one of the awards, earning his place at Eton with the brightest and best in the United Kingdom. They would miss him, of course, miss him terribly, but what an opportunity.

Baird never told them how homesick he was. He never told them how he was mocked for his thick Glasgow accent, or what some of the other boys called his *rustic ways*, which infuriated him, because it wasn't as if he was born under a rock. He was no more rustic than they, and at least he had proper manners and knew better than to bully other lads for things they couldn't help or change.

Some of the bullying eased when Baird picked up a hockey stick. A growth spirit was putting size on him, and he already had speed. The fact that he also excelled in rugby and rowing meant that he was just as strong in sports as he was in the classroom. It was during the Lenten season when Baird and Alec met. They were playing on different teams but knew of each other, and Alec was the one to approach Baird and introduce himself.

Baird didn't know what to think about Viscount Sherbourne. Why would the future earl want to be friends with him? Was it a joke? A prank? Had someone put Sherbourne up to it?

But no, Alec was just as miserable as Baird—for different reasons, though. While Baird couldn't wait for school holidays to return home, Alec dreaded the visits to Langley Park. Alec had no one at home, and it was excruciating returning. Baird loved his family, they were a proper family, and he told Alec he was always welcome at the MacLaurens. They didn't have a big house. They didn't have a lot of money, but they had a lot of love. Soon Alec was going home with Baird for holidays, and over the years, the boys developed an unbreakable bond.

They stayed close at university and supported each other through their twenties—Alec at Langley Investments, working beneath his cold and exacting father, and Baird becoming a lawyer, first earning his degree in Scots Law, and then studying for the tests that would allow him to practice law in England as well. Baird was hired immediately by one of London's biggest firms and he spent the next five years representing international cases, traveling more than he was home. The money was excellent, though, and he sent as much as he could to his parents every month, allowing them to retire, and pay off their house, and buy a new car.

Baird probably wouldn't have switched his focus to family law if it weren't for his father's heart attack. Baird realized he was never home to see his parents and there was an intriguing opportunity for him in Scotland that would allow him to split his time between Glasgow and Edinburgh. Ready for change, and a lot less international travel, he took the position with the prominent Scots firm, which proved to be a good decision, at least financially. Switching to family law was even more lucrative than corporate law, allowing him to pay off his parents mortgage so his father could retire. Baird had bought property himself, living in one and leasing out the others. Because money had been such a concern when he was growing up, he knew he should be grateful it wasn't an issue anymore, but there were times he felt like he'd sold his soul to the devil. There was no joy in learning all the ugly hateful things people did to each other—said to each other—when their marriage failed.

Baird didn't fall asleep until midnight. When he woke and saw that it was not even six o'clock, he tried to fall back asleep, but sleep wouldn't come. Perhaps the best thing to do was go for a run and work through all the thoughts and the worries he never shared with others.

He was the one people went to with their problems. He didn't ever want to be a burden. He didn't want others to feel pressured or troubled, and so he kept everything inside, and for the most part, it worked.

This morning was different, but the run would clear his head. It always did.

ELLA WOKE TO the smell of coffee. There were few things she loved in the world as much as that first cup of coffee, and she threw back the covers and tugged on sweatpants over her pajama pants, adding a sweatshirt over her sleepshirt before going down to the kitchen to see if there was any coffee left for her.

Baird was in the tiny kitchen standing before the tiny sink, in thick fleece sweatpants looking out the kitchen window, so completely lost in thought that Ella froze on the threshold unwilling to interrupt him. She also couldn't look away from him, either. From the dark hair curling at his nape, to his strong slightly hooked nose, to the powerful width of his shoulders, he was an incredibly appealing man.

As if realizing she was there, Baird glanced her way. The corner of his mouth tugged into a smile. "Cara said you liked coffee."

Ella nodded, suddenly shy. She raked her fingers through her tangled hair. "My brothers used to say I respond to coffee the way dogs do to bacon."

Baird's smile widened. "I thought your brothers were nicer than that."

"Ben is," she said. "But the other two, Tom and Mark, were trying to impress you."

"I thought Ben was your brother in Dubai."

"He is."

"Why is he the nicest?"

"He's a good listener, he's nonjudgmental and he's patient. I don't know how he ended up with so much patience. No one else in the family is."

"Was his advice good?"

"No. I hated it. It generally involved asking people for forgiveness and then doing good deeds to prove you'd grown and changed."

"Penance."

"More or less."

Baird's smile was lopsided. "So, why go to him?"

"Because he was a good person, and never made you feel dumb for making what was essentially dumb mistakes." She remembered some of the dumber things she did, like sneaking out her freshman year of high school to meet Jay, her brother Mark's friend, but Jay didn't have her best interests in mind, and Ella had to call Ben to come save her from the situation. Ben wasn't exactly kind to Jay, but Ella thought Jay deserved the bloody nose.

"Sounds like you were close," Baird said.

"Cara and Ben were my favorites, not that you're supposed to have favorites, but I always felt protective of Cara, and Ben was always keeping an eye out for me." She hesitated. "I was really sad when he went to MIT for school. I had a feeling that once he moved away, he'd never move back, and I was right. Even before he'd graduated, he was hired to work for a firm in the Middle East, and he's been there ever since—" She broke off. "Sorry, that's a lot of information before you've even had your coffee."

Baird removed the plastic top that rested on the ceramic mug. "I've had a cup already. This one was for you. I was going to take it to you upstairs. Your sister warned me it might be the only way to get you out of bed."

Ella grimaced. "She knows me so well."

"So, what are your plans today? I imagine you'll be spending most of it with Cara."

"I imagine so. We didn't really talk about today, but it's probably going to be a lazy day." Ella sipped her coffee. It was hot and strong, just the way she liked it. "And you?"

"Just work," Baird answered. "Unless someone here at the house needs me to run an errand. I've offered my services to both Mrs. Booth and Mrs. Johnson."

"That's nice of you." She started to take her coffee and then remembered last night's soccer match. "So, who won the game?"

"Not my team," Baird said. "But my team's loss made Mrs. Johnson happy."

Ella grinned. "You sound like a good loser."

"I'm not. But I wasn't going to let Mrs. Johnson know I was upset. Then she'd only gloat."

"I haven't even been here a day, and I'm learning so much about everyone."

"Mrs. Johnson, fierce football fan. Baird MacLauren, poor loser.

Ella laughed. "I better go dress but thank you again for the coffee."

His eyes met hers. "My pleasure."

Heat filled her, heat and fizz, and she suddenly felt lightheaded. "Are you coming up to the house for breakfast?'

"No. I've already had some eggs. I'm good for now."

"Okay." Ella turned around and climbed the stairs, heart thumping with every step, hand trembling from too much adrenaline, making the cup wobble in her hand.

Baird MacLauren was still too handsome, too fascinating, and too physically appealing. Suddenly that mad passionate kiss last August didn't seem so long ago.

CARA WAS NOT in the best mood when Ella entered the bedroom. The blue velvet curtains were only partially opened and Cara was sitting in a chair, not in bed, a tea pot next to her, the cozy still on the pot, the teacup empty.

"What's wrong?" Ella asked Cara, noting that the scones on Cara's plate hadn't been touched, either.

"Alec's not answering my calls."

"Maybe he's just busy."

"No. He always calls me back and it's been hours."

"When was the last time you talked to him?"

"Yesterday, early afternoon. It was just a brief call. He said he'd call me before bed. He always calls me before bed, but he didn't last night, and he hasn't called this morning." Cara glanced at her watch. "It's almost ten. We usually talk around seven. It's our routine."

"Do you think he's sick? Could he have a bug?"

"He'd still call or text me. He'd say he felt terrible, or something. But there's been no communication at all. It's not normal." Her eyes filled with tears. "I keep wondering if I did something to make him angry—"

"I'm sure you haven't," Ella interrupted, kneeling in front of Cara's chair. "Maybe he's just so busy getting ready to come home for the holidays that he's lost track of time."

"Impossible. That would never happen, not with Alec He'd never be so irresponsible."

"So, what do you think has happened?"

"I don't know." Cara's voice broke. "What if he's... hurt. Or..." She reached up to wipe away a tear that was falling. "Or worse."

"I'm sure nothing has happened to him. Someone would have alerted you. The police, or a hospital." Ella took Cara's hand. "Have you asked Baird? Perhaps he's heard something."

"I did. Baird said he spoke to Alec yesterday, just before dinner, but he hasn't heard anything today."

Ella was silent, processing. Maybe something had happened to Alec. Maybe there had been an accident. "Why don't we ask Baird to call Alec this morning, and if Alec doesn't answer, you or Baird or someone could call the office and check on Alec." Ella paused. "Maybe there has been some kind of stock market thing, maybe the market has crashed, or maybe there's something else demanding Alec's focus. Let's stay calm and let Baird help figure this out. Next to you, he's the one who knows Alec best. He can get us the answers we need."

"Go talk to him then. I need to know."

"You don't want breakfast? Some eggs or oatmeal?"

Cara shook her head. "I'm too upset to eat."

Ella walked quickly back to the cottage where she found Baird at the simple dining table, computer out, papers spread around him.

"That was fast," he said, sitting back in his chair.

"She didn't want breakfast, couldn't eat. She's a mess." Ella pulled out a chair and sat down at the table. "Cara said she hasn't talked to Alec since early afternoon yesterday. She said they always talk every night, before they go to bed, but he didn't call her last night, and he didn't answer when she called him. She phoned again this morning and nothing." Ella looked at Baird. "Have you talked to him today?"

"Just briefly."

"So, he's alive?"

"Yes."

"Not bloodied and lying in a ditch somewhere."

"No."

"Why is he avoiding Cara then?"

"He's not avoiding Cara—"

"He's not speaking to her, Baird. Just you."

"He's barely speaking to me as well. I just happen to know what's going on so I'm someone he can talk to."

Ella studied him for a long moment from across the table. "This doesn't sound good."

"It's not good." He pushed up from the table. "I'm going to take the dogs for a walk. Want to go?"

"Now?"

"That's why Alec called. He wanted to be sure the dogs were getting out twice a day, and I promised him I'd handle it." He reached for his coat. "We can talk while we walk. It'll be easier than just sitting here."

Ella nodded, trying not to let her imagination run away with her. "I'm ready when you are."

At the house, the dogs were thrilled to be leashed for a walk. Baird took the young labs while Ella took Lady's leash. The morning was clear and crisp, the sky a lovely blue. They walked in silence for several minutes. Ella bit her tongue, waiting for Baird to share what he knew. She didn't have to wait very long.

"There's something Cara needs to know that she does not know," Baird said after a minute. "It's not my place to tell her, and it's not your place to tell her, but there's a reason Alec isn't here and it's serious."

Ella swallowed around the lump filling her throat, anxiety knotting her chest. "Is he having an affair?"

"No. *No.* Absolutely not. This is about business, his business." Baird exhaled, his gaze fixed on the gravel road winding before them. "Something has happened. It's why he's been in London, which is why he might not be here for the party, which is why I don't think there should be a party."

"And you can't tell me?"

"I don't know. That's what I'm trying to figure out. On one hand I think it would help explain Alec's absence, but I worry you'll tell Cara and then it's just going to create drama no one needs."

"You can trust me. You're not the only one who can keep a secret."

His lips curved. "I do believe that was a direct hit."

Ella pushed a loose strand of hair back, tucking it behind her ear. "The point is you don't want me to say anything to Cara."

"Yes. This is Alec's business—literally his business—and when Alec wants Cara to know, he'll tell her. He just isn't in the right headspace at the moment."

"Is that why he's not talking to her?"

"I don't know about that. We haven't been talking in depth. He just gives me brief updates. All I know, with regards to Cara, is that he's not trying to hurt her. If anything, he's trying to protect her." Baird glanced at Ella, brow furrowed. "He's afraid a shock with his situation will deeply upset her, causing a miscarriage. I don't think his news will jeopardize her pregnancy, but who am I to weigh in? I'm not a doctor. I'm not her husband. I'm not the father of the babies. Alec is trying to do his best and he needs our support, all of our support."

Baird's words filled Ella with foreboding. There was no

light in his eyes, no levity in his voice. He looked somber, and so deeply troubled that it made her gut cramp, as if she'd swallowed a handful of nails. "I promise I won't say anything to Cara."

The younger dogs were frustrated by their slow pace, and Baird unhooked their leashes so they could go run, the estate being huge, the dogs could dash about without getting into harm.

Lady was happy just walking at Ella's side so Ella left Lady on her leash. "Is Alec in danger?"

"No, not that kind of danger. He won't be arrested, either, but he is in trouble. His firm is in trouble, and it's a family firm, one that was started by his grandfather decades ago. He's worried that it might end up in the news, and so he's calling the clients that have been impacted, letting them know what's happened and what he's doing about it. He believes they deserve to know the facts—the truth—before anyone else."

She suddenly felt like she'd heard this story before, felt as if it was one that played out wherever there was wealth and those who managed money. "Has he lost their money?"

"Not Alec, but one of the senior vice presidents at Langley investments, one of the most senior vice presidents, has apparently embezzled millions of pounds. Not just from the clients, but from Alec as well. Alec discovered it a week ago, saw inconsistencies in some of the accounts, funds not matching with records and began digging in more deeply, and that's when he discovered his most trusted right hand had been stealing for the past two years."

"No," Ella whispered.

Baird nodded. "It was never a lot at one point at one time. Twenty thousand here, fifty thousand there, but it added up and when Alec asked his senior executive to help him investigate, not realizing that James Phelps was the culprit, it gave James time to disappear, and he's vanished."

"With the money."

"With the money," Baird's agreed, voice deepening. "Alec is breaking the news to his clients today. He's personally calling each and explaining the situation, hoping to speak to everyone before it's headline news."

"I can't believe it. Alec is so cautious, so careful, so conscientious."

"It is devastating. It impacts him, the firm, the family's reputation."

"And you said Alec has also lost money?"

"A significant amount, yes."

"Just one more reason there can't be a party here on Saturday. The news could break Friday, or Saturday—"

"Or tonight."

"There's no way we can put Alec through that. It would be excruciating." Ella's stomach churned, nauseous just thinking about it. No wonder Alec wasn't home. She also understood now why Baird was here. Alec was entrusting Baird to take care of his family until he could return. "We have to cancel the party. There's no excuse now, not when we know what Alec's dealing with."

"I agree. But your sister has been adamant."

"That's because she doesn't know the truth, and if she knew the truth, she'd put a stop to the party immediately." Ella stopped walking and Baird did, too. They faced each other beneath the dappled shade of the stately oak trees.

"But as we've agreed," Ella continued, "we can't tell her, so we just have to make the decisions that need to be made. We have to go back to the house and talk with the staff. We need to enlist their help and get the event cancelled while we have time to get the word out."

They'd walked down a road and passed a number of cottages before coming to the end.

"If you continue through the gates," Baird said, pointing to where the road disappeared through tall gates, "you are just outside Bakewell. Continue along the path that follows the road and you'll be in town in no time."

"No excuse for me to get lost then," she answered.

"None at all." Baird whistled, calling for Milo and Albert, and the labs came running. They turned around then and began the walk to the house.

When the house came into view, Ella removed Lady's leash, too, and all three dogs went bounding up the sweeping drive toward the mudroom door before Lady stopped and turned to look at the humans.

In the mudroom, Baird hung up the leashes and washed

his hands in the small bathroom.

"Shall we gather the troops?" Ella asked, washing her hands next. "Come up with our battle plan?"

He nodded. "I think so."

ELLA AND BAIRD joined Mrs. Johnson and Mrs. Booth in the kitchen. Mrs. Booth had made a pot of tea, and they sat on the counter stools around the oversized marble island to talk. "Alec is in a situation," Ella said bluntly. "Cara doesn't know about it yet, but from what Baird shared, there is no way Alec and Cara can entertain neighbors on Saturday. Baird and I agree that the party must be cancelled, or at the very least, postponed, but we don't have the guest list and we're unable to take the next steps without you."

"Her ladyship shouldn't be entertaining anyone," Mrs. Booth said, voice firm. "I've been worried about hosting a party here, on top of Lord Sherbourne's family arriving."

"Mrs. Booth and I can split the guest list," Mrs. Johnson added. "If we divide and conquer, we should have it done by noon."

"We need to break the news to Cara," Baird added. "And then maybe take her out, do something to help distract her. She hasn't been downstairs once since I arrived, and a change of scenery and fresh air would lift her spirits."

Ella nodded. "I bet she'd like that. I'll go talk to her. I'll tell her that we've decided—that *I've* decided—it's not in her best interest to try to entertain people, not when she's supposed to be taking it easy. She won't like it. Cara looks sweet but is incredibly stubborn. But I know how to make her listen."

"Oh?"

"I'll threaten to call Mom and Cara would hate that. She hates when Mom fusses over her."

"And you don't?"

Ella shrugged. "They never really fussed over me. I never caused any problems. I just did what I needed to do."

"I can't imagine Cara causing problems."

"Not the way you think, but she had some struggles growing up and my parents were slow getting her the help she needed. Once they understood the issue, everything changed, but they've felt guilty ever since, all their talking and fretting over her.

LADY FOLLOWED ELLA up the beautiful curving Georgian staircase to the second floor but when Ella knocked on the bedroom door Lady went back down the stairs.

Cara was just returning to bed from the bathroom, and she smiled as Ella entered the room. "He called," she said, relief in her voice. "We just talked. Alec has a big project and he's trying to get it done so he can get home."

"So, you two are okay?"

"Yes." Cara sat down on the edge of her bed and pulled her robe close to her bump. "I'm sorry I was so dramatic earlier. I'm becoming so emotional. I hate it."

"Probably the pregnancy hormones, but no one minds."

"I do."

"At least you feel better now."

Cara nodded. "Much better."

"Good, because we need to talk about this weekend." Ella sat down next to her sister on the bed. "I am worried about Saturday's party. Baird and I have been discussing we agree this isn't the time for you to be entertaining—"

"You and Baird agree on something?"

Ella smiled ruefully. "Yes. Shocking, isn't it?"

"Not really. You both have the hots for each other—"

"Okay, that's not a conversation we're having. But Baird and I do think that in light of Alec having such a big ... project ... at work, he's not going to want to come home and have to socialize for hours here. I remember you saying that Christmas isn't the easiest time of year for him, and with everything you two have going on, please postpone the party. Wait until the new year. Maybe even until the babies arrive. Your neighbors and friends would rather you have a healthy pregnancy than take risks now. Cancel the party. Or I will."

Cara's smile faded. "You're serious."

"Yes, and you should be, too." Ella paused, let her words sink in. "So, do I have your permission to cancel the party?

Because the sooner we get the word out, the better."

"Fine. But no mention of my pregnancy, okay? Just in case…"

"I promise." Ella paused. "And one more thing."

"What?" Cara asked darkly.

"Would you like to go out for a drive? Baird thought you'd enjoy a change of scenery."

Cara stood. "Yes, yes, please. I'd love that more than anything. Did he say where we'd go?"

"Not yet."

"While I get dressed, see what he thinks about driving to the Peaks. I'd love for you to see some of the National Park."

Chapter Four

Baird carried Cara down to his car, with her protesting the entire way, asking if he needed to stop and rest, or if his back was hurting.

Baird did groan once or twice for her benefit, which made her laugh, and even Ella was smiling, glad to see Cara's mood so vastly improved.

It was a perfect day for a drive, too. There were no clouds in the sky and the bright winter sun painted the rolling hills and valleys shades of gold. Baird turned on music, a Scottish folk band, but he kept the volume low so they could talk, but no one seemed interested in talking. It was nice just to be out, soaking up the sun and the freedom of being away from the house.

Baird and Cara conferred about where to go and what to see, and after some discussion, Baird drove them through Wye Head and then Buxton before heading north to Winnats Pass.

"Alec brought me here last year," Cara said, pointing to the turnout she wanted Baird to take. "There is the most gorgeous view of the pass and limestone gorge if you get out of the car and walk a little bit. I'm not going to get out, but I want you to see it, Ella."

After forty-five minutes in the car, Ella was happy to get out and stretch her legs. The air was fresh, cold, and the wind whistled through the pass. The cold felt good, invigorating, and the rocky gorge was definitely worth the drive.

"I'm so glad you suggested this," Ella said to Baird as they walked to the overlook to take in the view. "Cara is already happier."

"I thought you might like a drive, too," Baird said, glancing at her. "You haven't seen much since you arrived."

"I wasn't expecting to be doing a lot of sightseeing. I just wanted to see Cara and make sure she's doing well, and except for the bedrest, she'd doing great." Ella chewed the inside of her lip. "I just wonder how she'll handle Alec's news when he tells her."

"They're a good couple, and good for each other. My gut says they will be fine."

Ella nodded, reassured by Baird's confidence.

"As you probably know, Alec has been through a lot," Baird added. "Alec was never the golden boy at Langley Investments. His dad was tough on him, but it didn't break Alec. It just made him stronger. Alec will get the firm through this. He's good at weathering storms."

"Cara is the same. She grew up feeling a lot of criticism and pressure, but she didn't let it get to her. She has a good head on her shoulders, and the most wonderful heart. Once

Alec tells her, it'll be better for him … for both of them."

"I agree."

Silence stretched, but it was strangely companionable. Ella liked it, glad not to feel adversarial with Baird.

"Do we need to talk about what happened at the wedding?" Baird asked abruptly, looking at her, his gaze briefly holding hers.

His question caught her off guard. "Do we?"

"It seems like we should. If not now, soon. There are a few things I'd like to clear up."

Up until that moment, Ella would have said yes, they definitely needed to talk about what happened at the wedding, but now hearing him say there were things he wanted to clear up made her heart fall. Would he apologize again? Would he bring up his girlfriend? Repeat how that kiss had been a terrible mistake. She shuddered inwardly, not ready for any of that.

"I'm not sure what you can say that will change what happened. I'm not sure I need to hear anything, either. Maybe we just put it behind us." Ella was grateful her voice was firm.

"Not trying to extract myself. I was there. You were there. And it was a pretty … intense … kiss."

Her insides somersaulted. "I thought so too, until you mentioned you had a girlfriend." Ella steeled herself. "*After* kissing me senseless. That wasn't fair. But then, some men play by their own rules."

"I do have my own rules, but they don't include taking advantage of anyone, much less my best friend's new sister-in-law. Because you're right, that wouldn't be fair, or cool."

She met his gaze. "Are there extenuating circumstances I'm not aware of? Are you going to blame your lapse on the romantic setting, the summer night, or something much more basic? The fact that you simply got carried away?"

"It was a romantic environment. It was a beautiful night. We did get carried away. But I was not in a relationship at the time. I wasn't cheating on anyone. I wouldn't do that. That's crossing the line."

"But you said—"

"I said I wasn't available," he interrupted flatly. "And emotionally I wasn't."

"But physically you were?"

"Physically ... it was one intense kiss. We had chemistry, but it was too much too soon. I wasn't ready to pursue anything with you, which is why I said I was sorry. I was sorry for leading you on."

"I wasn't expecting you to get down on one knee and propose. It was a kiss, a kiss I quite enjoyed until you ruined it by making it all seem ... sordid."

"Then I am sorry for that as well. It wasn't my intention."

Ella was so tired of his apologies. "Can we try never to discuss this again? You've successfully ruined that memory several times. Thank you."

His lips twitched. "You are so angry."

"I am." She faced him, temper blazing. "You are this gorgeous man, big, handsome, with the most delicious accent I've ever heard. Every time you talk, I melt a little bit, but then I listen to the things you're saying and it's maddening. I want to throw rocks at you. Next time you kiss a woman, and kiss her the way you kissed me, do not apologize. Do not say it was a mistake. Do not walk away leaving her alone, leaving her to feel bad. That was mean, and you don't strike me as someone who enjoys being mean." Ella didn't give him time to respond. She turned around and swiftly marched back to the car, wishing she hadn't gotten so upset, wishing she hadn't revealed just how badly he'd hurt her.

"What did you think?" Cara asked, as Ella opened the passenger door in the backseat. "Beautiful, isn't it?"

"Yes. I'm so glad we drove up here."

"What happened to Baird?"

"I think he's taking some pictures," Ella fibbed.

"But his phone is here."

Ella shrugged. "I don't know what's keeping him then."

BAIRD WATCHED ELLA walk away, her long red hair in a single plait down her back, arms swinging at her sides with military precision. She was furious. He wasn't sure what he felt—disappointment? Surprise?

Last August, he'd thought he was being a gentleman apologizing for his lapse in control, wanting to make amends for behavior that was out of character for him.

Baird didn't make out with women at parties. He didn't draw young women into the shadows and kiss them against boathouse walls, hands trapping her so he could better take and taste her mouth.

He certainly didn't seduce women related to Alec, and yet there he was, hours after the wedding, making love to Alec's new sister-in-law, feeling things he never felt, wanting things he never craved, desire so strong it had driven all rational thought from his head.

In the end, it might have just been a moment, or maybe thirty moments, who knew? But it would have gotten completely out of hand if he hadn't heard a voice ask if anyone had seen Ella. Baird didn't care who asked the question, he just knew they couldn't be discovered like this, in the dark, Ella pressed to the wall, his hands in her hair, his mouth claiming hers.

Certain they were about to be seen, he stepped backward and tugged on his tie. Ella was still in the shadows.

"I'm sorry." His voice came out deep, rough. His blood was still humming through him, his body tight, hard.

What an extraordinary moment, more than a moment. Part of him longed to scoop her up and take her to his room and finish what they'd begun. But reason was stirring, and there was no way he'd ever be able to look Alec in the eye if he did that.

No, it had to end here. He had to make this right.

"That was a mistake," he said gruffly. "It shouldn't have happened—"

She made a sound. It confused him. Was she laughing? Or…

Flustered, he said something else, trying to smooth it all over, when part of him still felt drugged by the heat and need.

She'd been fire in his arms. Kissing her knocked him sideways. She stirred emotions he didn't think he had, and even standing five feet apart, he felt her, the desire a living breathing thing.

Kissing her, touching her, holding her had been life changing. It had been the most physical, carnal, powerful need. Like oxygen, he had to have it.

But oxygen and fire were a deadly combination.

He walked away from her because he had to. If he stayed, he'd take her in his arms again and then it would be game over.

He returned to the party, and circulated for twenty minutes at the reception, speaking with friends of the Roberts, and then with Ben, Cara and Ella's brother. Ben had flown in from Dubai where he worked as an engineer, and Baird, who had clients in Dubai, found a lot in common with Ella's brother. They talked about their experiences in the UAE, and a person it turned out they both knew, until Ben was called away to dance with his mother.

Baird deliberated if he should circle the reception again or just return to his room.

He returned to his room and once there he stripped out of his tuxedo and dress shirt and showered. With a towel wrapped around his hips, he began to pack. He was going to leave in the morning, catch the late morning flight back to Heathrow and then book a new connecting flight to Edinburgh.

Now, here they were together again, and it was every bit as complicated as it had been in August.

He'd never met anyone who stirred him the way Ella did. He'd never met anyone he wanted like Ella. But there was no logic in the desire, and there was nothing Baird could see to explain the attraction. What did they have in common? Nothing. What goals did they share? None.

Yes, she was beautiful and fiery, spirited and passionate, but those weren't traits he wanted in a partner. He wasn't looking for heat. He wasn't interested in an intense physical connection. He wanted someone steady, someone independent and successful, someone like Fiona, who had been content with him, content without a marriage certificate, content without children, until the day she confessed, she wasn't.

❄

THE WINDOWS OF the car were beginning to steam up. Ella was fine with it. She didn't want to see Baird or be trapped in the car with him any longer, but Cara had been watching for him compulsively. "He's returning now," she said happily.

Ella closed her eyes and pressed a fist to her forehead, wishing she had wings and could just fly home.

She and Baird shouldn't have discussed the wedding. It would have been better to pretend the kiss never happened. After all, it was just a kiss, and Baird truly didn't figure in her goals or future. She just had to find a way to remain detached. Distance was the key.

But as Baird opened the car door the very energy changed, charging the molecules with something alive, something she couldn't define.

He might pretend to be calm and rational, but she knew better. He wasn't the quiet logical man he presented to the world. Beneath his rugged virile exterior was a volcano—hot, dangerous, molten.

She shouldn't want it, or him, but stupidly, she did.

"Where to now?" Baird asked, starting the car.

"What if we continue the way we're going with a stop at Monsal Head, another of the most photographed spots in the Peak District? It shouldn't be that far from here, and near the car park there's a little place we could get tea and cake," Cara added. "It would be a nice break before returning home. Besides, I would be thrilled to use the lavatory."

"Sounds good," Baird said, shifting into gear.

Before he backed out, his gaze went to the rearview mirror and collided with Ella's. Something passed between them ... an awareness, a knowing, a connection neither of them wanted but couldn't shake.

Ella swallowed hard and looked away, wondering if she'd imagined that raw intensity in his eyes, wondering if she'd imagined the fire in his kiss. Was she lost in a world of fiction? Was she making up things in her head now?

No. She wasn't. She couldn't be.

Baird was the mystery. Baird was the one who didn't want to feel. But he was also the one who'd set her on fire.

THEY STOPPED AT the teahouse, and it was the perfect break before they returned to the car to head to Langley Park, which was only fifteen minutes away.

If Cara sensed any tension between Ella and Baird she ignored it, talking about all her favorite places Ella should see in the next two weeks, including a train trip to Bath after Boxing Day, if she felt like making a day trip. Or better yet, staying overnight if she could find an inexpensive place to stay since there was so much to see and do.

"Jane Austen lived in Bath," Cara added, as if she needed to convince Ella to make the trip. "Last summer, before the wedding, Alec took me to Bath for the weekend. We stayed at the Royal Crescent Hotel and Spa, and visited Jane Austen's museum, the Pump House, the Upper Assembly Rooms. I loved it, and you've read all her books, while I've only seen the movies, so with your thesis and all, you'll be in heaven."

"That's actually a good idea," Ella said, thinking a few days off on her own might just be what she needed, unless, of course, Baird would be departing Langley Park once Alec returned. She hoped he would. With the party cancelled, there was no reason for him to stay on. "Let's see how Christmas goes, and if it works out, I'll make the trip. It's not terribly far by train, is it?"

"Four and a half, to five hours," Baird said, "plus two to three train changes."

The distance didn't worry Ella, but two to three train changes? That sounded like a lot. "I'll think about it," she said.

"Or maybe Baird could take you," Cara suggested. "If he has time."

"He doesn't," Ella said quickly, stomach doing a somersault. She avoided making eye contact as well, determined to avoid engaging. "He has a lot of work. He's been focused every evening and morning at the cottage, and I'm not going to disrupt his work more than I already have." She dabbed her mouth with her napkin, wiping away the delicious, clotted cream. "Should we head back soon? I know how much you love your naps, Cara."

RELIEF FLOODED ELLA as Baird pulled through Langley Park's impressive front gates, and then traveled down the winding road with the border of ancient trees. Here and there, the trees would give way, teasing views of the great house. It wasn't until they drew close to the house, they could see a car in the driveway.

"That's Aunt Emma's car," Cara said, leaning forward as Baird slowed and parked. "Which means Aunt Dorothy is also here."

Baird turned the ignition off. "I didn't think they were to come until tomorrow."

Cara smiled wryly. "They arrived early last year as well. I wondered if they'd show early this year, too. Fortunately, everything's ready. I do wish Alec was here, though."

"I know you miss him," Ella said gently. "But he'll be home this weekend."

"He should have been home already." Cara's voice dropped and then she added firmly, "But you're right, it won't be long now, and it'll be extra wonderful being together after so much time apart."

Baird came around the car and opened the passenger door for Cara, but Cara refused to be carried into the house, saying it was silly to be carried such a short distance, and the last thing she wanted was to have Alec's family ask questions or fuss.

Ella walked next to Cara as they entered through the grand front door into the soaring entry with the curving staircase topped by the glass dome. Sunlight warmed the marble floor, reflecting off the pale walls with the huge oil canvases. From the back of the house, they heard the dogs bark, and then Mrs. Johnson shushed them.

The door to the drawing room was open and Cara entered first. The drawing room, also called the green room by staff, looked particularly distinguished at Christmas with the holly and green garlands hung above the doors, the mantle adorned with more of the same greenery and tall white taper candles which would be lit at night.

The large, elegant room had two seating areas and Alec's great uncle and two aunts were at the end of the room with the magnificent Christmas tree, having tea under the watchful eye of Mrs. Booth.

"Uncle Frederick!" Cara cried as they entered the room, walking quickly to his side and kissing his cheek. "This is a surprise. I didn't see your car out front."

Alec's great Uncle Frederick had to be eighty, if not older, and he attempted to rise to greet her, but Cara patted his arm. "Please don't get up," she said. "I am curious how you got there, though."

Frederick glanced at the aunts. "Emma offered to pick me up. I refused. I didn't want to put her out—"

"So I picked him up anyway," Emma replied. "I will not be outmaneuvered."

Ella liked this group already. "I'm Ella," she said, stepping forward, "Cara's sister. I've heard so much about all of you and am very happy to be here for Christmas."

Cara quickly introduced Alec's family. "Uncle Frederick, Aunt Emma and her sister-in-law, Aunt Dorothy." She then turned to Baird. "I'm sure you all remember Baird MacLauren, Alec's best friend from Eton."

There were greetings and handshakes between Baird and Frederick Sherbourne. Baird went to kiss both of the aunts on their cheeks. He and Dorothy spoke for a moment, reminiscing about Christmas in Edinburgh as her late husband had been from Scotland.

Seeing that everyone was settling in, Mrs. Booth rose. "I shall go see about getting a fresh pot of tea and more refreshments, although I suspect Mrs. Johnson already has it all in hand."

She bustled out and Cara shifted seats, taking Mrs. Booth's chair so she could better see everyone. "So, what has everyone been discussing?" Cara asked, smiling at everyone. "What have I missed?"

"What do you think?" Uncle Frederick demanded. "Terrible, terrible news today. What has the world come to?"

Cara frowned, puzzled. "What has happened? I haven't been paying attention to the news. It's always so depressing."

"Frederick," Emma said under her breath. "We agreed."

"Yes, but maybe she can explain it to me. I don't understand," Frederick's voice sharpened.

"That's not her concern," Emma retorted, her stern gaze locking with Frederick's. "Alec said. Surely you remember that?"

Cara glanced around the room, eyes clear, watchful. "What are you hiding from me, Aunt Emma?" She looked at Dorothy and lifted her brow. "Aunt Dorothy, will you tell me?"

Dorothy held up her hands. "I know nothing."

"Someone knows something," Cara said. "Will no one tell me?"

Mrs. Johnson appeared then, carrying a tray with more teacups, a fresh teapot, and plates with small sandwiches and scones. Her arrival was a distraction and Ella was pleased to see one of the aunts, she wasn't sure which, take on hostess duties, pouring tea for everyone and passing around the refreshments.

So, they knew, Ella thought, watching Alec's elderly relatives. They must have gotten a call from Alec this morning, and then all jumped in the car and raced here.

Poor Cara, she didn't need this, but thankfully Emma was taking charge and shutting down Frederick's complaints. Hopefully, Alec would be home soon, and he'd explain everything to Cara.

"We had a lovely drive today," Ella said, taking control of the conversation to prevent it swinging back around to Alec and what was happening at work. "Cara, where did we go again? Winnart's Pass?"

"Winnat," Emma corrected. "That's a beautiful spot but it can be cold. Was the wind blowing terribly?"

"It was brisk," Ella said. "But it felt good. I had no idea that Bakewell was part of the Peak National Forest—"

"Not Forest," Emma corrected again. "Park. And yes, Bakewell and quite a number of villages are in the Park."

"You know Sheffield is in the Park, but not Buxton," Frederick said. "That's because when the boundaries were drawn Buxton was considered too big, what with the quarries and all."

The aunts and Frederick began to discuss Bakewell as they knew it when they were younger, and Ella relaxed, glad that Alec's family had found something to discuss with so much energy. Ella glanced at her sister who was smiling but also beginning to look sleepy. Ella was so glad Baird had taken Cara out today. Cara had needed the outing and Ella was glad to see some of the places Cara had seen last Christmas.

After twenty more minutes discussing the quarries and village growth, Frederick sat back in his chair. "I could use a short rest," he announced, "before dinner."

Dorothy nodded. "I think everyone could." She smiled at Cara, expression soft. "You look tuckered out, my dear."

"Does she?" Emma turned her attention to Cara. "I think she has excellent color. I don't see any fatigue."

"Well, I wouldn't mind a nap," Cara said, blushing. "But only if you might be resting, too."

Dorothy's eyes narrowed and her lips curved. "I'm wondering if you have news for us."

Cara ducked her head, and Emma and Dorothy exchanged glances.

"I can carry you up," Baird said, rising. "You're not supposed to put too much weight on your ankle for another day."

"What's wrong with your ankle?" Frederick asked.

"It's just a little sprain," Ella said, getting to her feet.

Dorothy looked concerned. "How will you manage at the party Saturday?"

Cara rubbed her temple. "About the party—"

"It's been cancelled," Ella said quickly.

"Postponed," Cara said. "Until the new year."

"Does this have to do with Phelps?" Uncle Frederick demanded, cane tap-tapping the floor.

Cara turned to Baird. "What about Phelps?"

"Nothing," Baird said, swinging her into his arms. "You're not to fret. Alec has done nothing wrong and everything right. Now let me heave your demanding self up the stairs. It's a chore, but I've been refreshed with sandwiches and tea and am feeling up to the challenge, although a challenge it will be."

Cara smiled, happy to be diverted. "Not sure you have sufficient strength. I think you ate only two of those cucumber sandwiches."

"You cast aspersions on this frame?" Baird said in mock

outrage. "I will have you know I am twice as strong as your husband, and twice as handsome."

Cara laughed, just as Baird intended. They were still bantering back and forth as Baird carried her from the room and up the stairs.

For a moment there was just silence and then Dorothy sighed, distressed. "She doesn't know, does she? About Phelps stealing from the clients?"

Ella shook her head. "I only know because Baird needed me to help convince Cara that a party wasn't a good idea, not when Alec is going through so much right now."

"She should know," Emma answered, setting her teacup down. "She'd want to know."

"I am sure Alec will tell her as soon as he returns," Ella answered. "He's trying to protect her."

"He certainly didn't try to protect us," Frederick said. "But I suppose there is no easy way to break that kind of news. It's distressing losing money—"

"We've all lost money," Emma cut him short. "Everyone in the family has. All of Langley clients have. But that's not why we're here. It's Christmas."

"We should buoy Cara's spirits," Dorothy added. "And once Alec returns, lift his as well. Cara is not responsible for what happened in London and should not be made to feel uncomfortable."

"I never said she was responsible," Frederick snapped. "But I think she would want to be part of the conversation."

"She will want to be part of the conversation once Alec tells her what's happened," Ella said. "But Alec is shielding her from anything stressful right now. It's not good for her."

"She's pregnant, isn't she?" Dorothy breathed.

Ella hesitated, trying to find the right words. "There might be some news to share with you once Alec is back."

Frederick banged his cane again. "It seems as if there's an awful lot of secrets. Can't say this. Don't discuss that. For goodness' sake, it's almost like the old days, when we couldn't discuss anything in the family. I thought times had changed."

Ella bit her lip to hide her smile. She rather liked Great Uncle Frederick, even if he was grumpy today. Cara had said he was a lovely older man and they had grown quite close in the past year. "I am going to go check on my sister," she said, getting to her feet, "but before I do, is there anything I can help with? Anything I can do to help you settle in?"

"No, no." Emma waved her hand. "Frederick and I both grew up here. We know where everything is."

BAIRD HAD DINNER with the aunts and Uncle Frederick while Ella kept Cara company. Cara didn't want to be upstairs anymore, but she also didn't want to be carried. They ate dinner on trays in chairs in front of the pretty marble fireplace and then Ella picked up a book on the shelf and read while Cara took a shower, wanting to be available in case anything happened.

Fortunately, nothing happened, and Cara emerged from the adjoining bathroom wrapped in a huge towel, her hair in a messy knot on top of her head. "I've been reading about bedrest during pregnancy," Cara said, rifling through a dresser drawer for pajamas. "A lot of doctors don't believe in it anymore, saying it doesn't help, and in fact, might make everything worse. You can't go through a whole pregnancy lying around. It's not healthy. You don't want a woman to give birth after losing too much muscle tone."

"But your doctor wants you on bedrest," Ella said calmly.

"Yes. I'm just thinking this is a bit extreme—me not doing anything, not walking even down my own stairs. I understand not going on arduous hikes and horseback riding, I can see why rock climbing is out, but stairs? Come on. This is absurd."

"You have cabin fever," Ella said as Cara disappeared back into the bathroom. "It will pass."

"It's not just boredom," Cara answered. "I'm used to being active. I like being active. I like exercise. Time moves way too slowly when you're stuck in bed."

"When do you see the doctor again?"

"Mid-January. The twelfth, I think." Cara emerged from the bathroom in her flannel pajamas, a hairbrush in her hand. She pulled the scrunchie from her long hair and began to brush it. "There's no reason I can't go up and down the stairs here. It's just a single flight."

"Well, it's not a normal flight of stairs. Your single flight is equal to two flights anywhere else. It's what? Forty steps?" She stood up and motioned for Cara to take her place. "Come sit. I'll brush your hair. It's gotten long.

"I haven't had it cut in ages," Cara said, sitting down. She closed her eyes as Ella ran a hand down her hair, smoothing it. "You used to brush my hair when you were little."

Ella took the brush from her sister. Once Cara was settled, Ella lifted the long mass and brushed the ends. "Half the time I'd get the brush tangled." Ella laughed, remembering. "Then Mom would have to come save your hair from the brush. Remember that one time Mom couldn't get the brush out? She had to cut some of your hair. You were very calm. If I remember right, I was the one crying. I felt terrible."

"It was just hair," Cara said shrugging. "I didn't really care."

"I did." Ella ran the brush from crown to the ends, glad to see Cara slowly relax. The last few weeks had to have been so stressful, and then with Alec gone on top of it, Cara needed some TLC. "I always wanted to have your hair. I didn't know why I had to have red hair."

"You don't still feel that way, do you?" Cara asked.

"No. Once I realized there were plenty of Disney princesses with red hair, I was good with it."

Cara laughed. "You loved Disney princesses far more than I did."

"I loved Merida from *Brave* best. Ariel was problematic for me. How could one give up your voice for legs? Your voice is important. You have to be known, have to be heard."

"And Merida made herself known. She was wild."

"She was strong." Ella hugged Cara. "Like you. You're strong. Brave. Always my hero."

Cara hugged Cara back. "You're brave, too."

Ella drew back a little. "Am I?"

Cara nodded, expression serious, and yet there was mischief in her eyes. "Oh yes. You're sharing a cottage with that fierce Baird MacLauren. Who knew you'd grow up to love Scottish men?"

Groaning in disgust, Ella pulled away. "I do not love Baird MacLean. We barely tolerate each other."

"Always the first step to true love."

"There's no love between us."

"Something must have happened.

"It doesn't matter."

"It does." Cara turned in her chair, looking up at Ella. "He's Alec's best friend, and one of my good friends—"

"That's good," Ella interrupted. "That's great. I'm not asking you to pick sides. There's no need for that. I'm not close with him, but that's okay. He's Alec and your friend. He doesn't need to be mine."

Chapter Five

Late the next morning Mrs. Booth had one of the younger staff set up tables in the green room, one at one end and the other off to the side of the fireplace. At the small table closer to the fireplace Uncle Frederick and Emma were playing cards, and Dorothy was at the game table at the far end of the room working on a jigsaw puzzle. Ella wandered through the room noting a few small packages had appeared beneath the Christmas tree and listened to Frederick and Emma laugh over a point won, before continuing to Dorothy at her puzzle table.

Dorothy looked up as Ella approached. "Mrs. Booth found a box of puzzles in one of the closets. This is a puzzle I gave to William years ago. Hoping there are no missing pieces. It only takes one missing piece to ruin a puzzle."

Ella leaned over the table to take a look at the picture on the box as Dorothy was only just beginning the puzzle and the pieces on the table were mostly green and reddish brown. The photo on the box was of two shaggy cow heads poking over a limestone wall.

"Highland cattle," Dorothy said. "My late husband and I

inherited my grandmother's property outside Edinburgh. It was a lovely little farm and when we could, we'd spend holidays there. I became very attached to the cows. They're huge but really the most lovely creatures."

"Was your grandmother Scottish?" Ella asked, sitting down and sorting pieces into different color piles.

"So, you and Emma aren't sisters? Or are you half-sisters?"

"We're sisters-in-law. My husband and her husband were brothers." Dorothy leaned across the table her voice dropping. "I'll tell you a secret. When I first married Cedric, Emma and I did not get on. She can be a bit bossy, and having been raised as Lady Emma, she used to act as if she was better than me."

"But you're so close now."

"Time and loss brought us together. We lost our husbands within four years of each other. My Cedric went first, and then her George." Dorothy picked up a piece, turning it in her fingers. "We still weren't close, but we began making an effort to see each other more often, at Christmas and Easter and such. It was when I lost my Michael—" Dorothy broke off, her voice quavering, and for a long moment she didn't speak, and then she carefully set the puzzle piece down.

"She came to stay with me then," Dorothy. "She arrived with a suitcase and didn't leave for months. Instead, she moved in, and she grieved with me. She'd always been jealous that I had a child when she didn't, but once Michael was gone, she apologized and we cried together. His death broke both of our hearts."

Ella blinked, her eyes burning with tears. "How old was your son when he died?"

"Twenty-seven. I had him late. Like Emma, I had trouble conceiving. And then at forty-one, I discovered I was pregnant, and it was a miracle. Cedric and I had given up, and just when I thought it would never happen, Michael arrived."

Dorothy let out a little cry as she found a place for a puzzle edge. She pressed it into place and then looked up at Ella and smiled. "I do love a good puzzle."

Ella smiled back, hiding how much her chest ached with bittersweet emotion. "I do, too."

BAIRD ENTERED THE green salon, his gaze sweeping the room. There she was, at a card table with Dorothy. Except for coffee this morning, Baird had seen little of Ella and he missed her. He wasn't interested in analyzing the emotion, he just wanted it the nagging empty feeling inside of him to go away.

Baird crossed the room and pulled out a chair at the puzzle table and sat down. "Need help?"

Ella lifted her head, her blue-green gaze meeting his. "I

wouldn't have thought you a puzzle fan," she said to him.

"We did a lot of puzzles in my family," he answered. "My dad wasn't a big fan of the telly, and limited it to a few hours a week, saying too much would ruin our brains. So, on Saturday nights we'd have family game night. Puzzles, cards, charades, board games. We still have game nights when we get together over the holidays."

"Are they together now?"

"Yes, but in Australia. Allison, my oldest sister, lives in Melbourne and in October she had a new baby and they've all gone over to meet him."

"Why didn't you go?" Ella asked.

"Alec had asked me to be here for the party."

Ella's expression turned incredulous. "You turned down a trip to Australia for a party here?"

He shrugged. "You came all the way from the Pacific Northwest for the party."

Her lips twitched as she fought a smile. "That's different."

"How so?"

"I'm Cara's sister."

"I'm Alec's best friend, and we're so close we might as well be brothers."

"Are you two bickering?" Dorothy asked, glancing up with a smile before adding to her edge, one side of the frame nearly complete. "Or is this how you young people flirt these days?"

Ella looked up, alarmed. "Not flirting," Ella said decisively.

Baird couldn't hide his smile. "There might be a little flirting, but Ella won't admit it."

Ella shot him a fierce look. Baird ignored it, but he was amused. He found Ella vastly entertaining.

They all worked on the puzzle for a good fifteen minutes, conversation limited to searching for specific puzzle pieces. Progress was being made but it was certainly slow. The thousand-piece puzzle was a challenging one with the entire center mostly the cows, with the gray stone wall below, green grass and green hills, and then just a sliver of blue sky.

Their focus was interrupted by Mrs. Johnson entering the drawing room with the afternoon tea tray. Excusing herself, Dorothy rose to go pour tea for Frederick and Emma leaving Baird and Ella alone.

Baird matched a gray piece to another cluster. "I hope you don't mind me helping with the puzzle," he said. "You two looked overwhelmed and I thought you'd appreciate help."

Ella's head slowly lifted. "You are desperate for attention today."

"Why are you so out of sorts?"

"I'm not. I was having a wonderful time working on the puzzle with Dorothy. You're the problem."

"I'm sorry."

"You're not," she snapped. "You enjoy being a nuisance."

She looked up at him then, her gaze bright, challenging. "Actually, nuisance isn't the right word. There are other adjectives better suited, like infuriating. Frustrating. Upsetting—"

"So, you are still angry with me."

She took one of the brown pieces from his side of the table, digging it out from the gray ones and with a little cry found a spot for the piece she'd just retrieved from his pile. "Why would I be angry?" she asked, already digging in his pieces for another gray one.

"You've been upset ever since we went on the drive yesterday. Our conversation about the wedding reception upset you."

"It did, yes. It would have been better not to have discussed it. It stirred up unpleasant memories." Ella successfully connected more pieces. "Memories I had worked very hard to forget." She looked at him again, eyebrows arching. "I hope we're not going to discuss *that* again. It didn't help yesterday and it won't help today."

"*That* being down by the boathouse."

She slammed a piece into the others using her fist. "*That* is what I'd like to do to your face."

She was impossible and outrageous which made him want to laugh. Her temper made him want to laugh. Her flashing eyes made him want to laugh. "So, we can't be friends," he said soberly to keep from laughing.

She sighed loudly, exasperatedly. "*No.*"

"But I've made you coffee now, twice."

She flipped a long red curl over her shoulder. "It was good but not that good."

Baird gave up holding the laughter in, and it rang out, a big belly laugh. She glanced up, a light in her eyes that made him think she wanted to smile, but she wasn't going to let herself, because he knew she was determined to be upset with him.

"We should be friends," he said matter of factly "I like you. I think you like me. Just a little. But a little is better than not at all."

Ella leaned across the table and lowered her voice. "What makes you think I like you? Even just a little bit?"

He leaned toward her, so they were quite close to each other's faces. And lips. His gaze dropped to her rosy mouth, her lips full and soft, and still so terribly tempting. "Because you like this between us. It's tense. It's uncomfortable. It's unpredictable." He looked back up into her eyes, the irises darker, the color deepening with emotion. "It's also exciting."

She was silent a long time, staring into his eyes, searching. "I don't trust you. You really hurt me."

He swallowed hard, caught off guard. He hadn't expected so much honesty, or the pain softening her voice. She sounded so vulnerable and young.

"I know you're not much for apologies," he said quietly. "Especially mine, but Eloise, I did not want to hurt you.

That's a promise. I enjoy teasing you, but I'm not teasing now."

She leaned away, and she glanced around the room before looking back at him. "Why did you call me Eloise?"

"It's your name."

"Yes, but no one calls me Eloise, not even my parents."

"Why not?"

"They don't like it."

"They gave you a name they don't like?"

"Yes. I'd like to think they'd been drinking but they weren't. They just couldn't agree on a name, and had been arguing about it for days, and were at an impasse. So, my dad suggested they rip up a baby book with girl names, crumple them up, put them in a hat. Whatever name Mom drew that would be my name."

"Now you're pulling my leg."

Her smile deepened and she shook her head. "No. And Eloise it was. Neither of them liked the name all that much so it quickly became Ella and I've been Ella ever since."

"But Eloise is a perfectly nice name."

"It is, if you're a German warrior."

Baird found her smile impossibly infectious. "Well, I like it. And even if it meant German cheese, I'd still like it."

Ella shook her head, but she was smiling, and in that moment, it meant everything to Baird.

"Do you think we should join them?" Ella asked, nodding at the three having tea together.

"Probably. I'm hoping there might be some shortbread today."

"Shall we go check out the tea tray?"

They crossed to the couch where everyone was sitting and pulled up chairs. Dorothy poured tea for both of them, and Emma asked Ella a question which allowed Baird to just listen and watch.

Ella was wearing a pale pink blouse, the shade almost the same pink as the bridesmaid dress she wore for the wedding. He'd liked her in blue at the cocktail party, but pink was her color. She looked ethereal, like a woodland fairy in the gauzy dress with wisps of fabric at her shoulders, the deep v-neckline setting off her pale skin and delicate shoulders. With her long red hair, the smattering of freckles across the bridge of her small, straight nose, and that mouth of hers—his imagination ran riot, picturing all the things he wanted, and all the things he shouldn't want. She was Alec's sister-in-law, she was young, she lived on a different continent … but that didn't seem to matter.

He'd done his best to avoid her during the weekend. He'd been at her side when circumstances required him to be present, but otherwise he did everything within his power to avoid her, hoping she'd lose some of her magic, that sparkle and vivacity that made him think she was from another world. But the magic didn't fade. The sparkle deepened, becoming a glow, light surrounding her, golden light illuminating her. And when she looked at him, her vivid sea blue eyes finding his, holding his, he felt as if he'd known her forever.

Was it possible he'd known her in a past life? Were there such things as past lives? The awareness and familiarity baffled him. He'd never had such a strong bond with a stranger.

But desire was a funny thing, it had no rules, no reason, no answers. It just was.

Baird's control snapped during the reception. He'd been on the dance floor one minute and then he was leading her out of the ballroom the next. Neither of them spoke as he drew her into the shadows of the boathouse, kissing her, forgetting everything but her.

Baird set his teacup down, harder than he intended. The cup rattled against the saucer and all eyes were on him.

"What's wrong?" Ella said, her smile faintly teasing. "Missing the shortbread?"

His pulse felt heavy. His body felt strange. If there weren't elderly aunts and an uncle watching, he might pull her onto his lap and kiss her, just to see if kissing her here would be as intense, and as consuming as it had been in the summer.

"I don't think Mrs. Johnson makes a lot of shortbread," Dorothy said. "But I can bake some later. I am very fond of my grandmother's recipe." She glanced around the room. "I made it last year with Emma and Cara. It didn't last long. I could double the recipe this year."

"I'd love to help if I could," Ella said. "I've never had homemade shortbread and it would be fun to see how it's made."

Dorothy nodded, pleased by Ella's offer. "I'll ask Mrs. Johnson if there's a good time we could use her kitchen."

"And maybe some American fudge," Frederick suggested. "Or am I the only one who enjoyed Cara's fudge last year?"

Emma frowned. "No, it was excellent, but we can't very well ask Cara to whip up a batch, can we?"

"I can make fudge. Cara and I use the same family recipe."

Emma nodded, satisfied with the solution. "Well, then, we'll all crowd into the kitchen later and do some holiday baking." She looked at Baird. "Will you be helping, or only eating?"

Baird knew they were all looking at him, waiting expectantly for an answer, and no one appeared more interested in his answer than Ella. "I can lend a hand," he said gruffly. "Crack eggs, measure, stir things. If that would be useful."

Ella's gaze met his, amusement in her lovely eyes. "A useful man is a wonderful thing."

And that settled that, Baird thought. He would be useful if it killed him.

LATE THAT AFTERNOON with Emma's peppermint creams,

Dorothy's shortbread, and Ella's American fudge cooling, everyone independently decided some quiet time was in order. The aunts went one way, Ella checked in on Cara who was napping, and Baird disappeared in another way.

Ella had far too much sugar and tea to nap, and she felt way too many feelings to just sit still. Having been given permission by both Mrs. Booth and Cara to explore the house, she decided she would see what she hadn't seen yet.

Taking the stairs to the second floor she went left at the landing instead of right. Everything on this side of the house was different, the hallways narrower, the materials heavier, tapestries and old gold framed oils. She walked until she reached a back staircase and went up a floor where there were more bedrooms, and found yet one more narrow curving staircase that went to what proved to be attic bedrooms, probably once used for servants, she imagined. It was freezing up there and the windows were small and high.

Ella went back down a floor and opened one of the closed doors. It was a small bedroom with dark paneling covering the walls and a lowered ceiling with the paneling, too. The ornate four-poster bed even featured a paneled top, the wood heavy and intricately carved. Dark red brocade curtains framed the narrow diamond paned windows, the bed's coverlet a red and gold silk, with a thick red border. She was most definitely in the old part of the house, and although it was chilly with no fire laid, it was a stunning room.

Ella closed the door, and then tried another closed door just two doors down. It was another bedroom, the paneling similar but only on two walls, the other wall a stone partially obscured by an enormous medieval tapestry. The colors were gold and blue in this bedroom, the blue a rich royal, curtains blue with heavy gold fringe. A small stained-glass picture depicting what looked like a coat of arms being held by a standing leopard and a unicorn was inset in the diamond paned windows.

A leopard and a unicorn?

Or was it a lioness and a dragon?

Ella moved closer to the circular stained-glass art and couldn't really decide what the creatures were, but the colors were stunning, and she could only imagine how beautiful it would look with the sun shining through.

Leaving the bedroom, she continued down the hall, discovering that it turned sharply right into another corridor, also long and narrow with no visible windows except for light coming in at the far end. She walked all the way to the end and discovered a relatively tall, narrow window inset into narrow circular stairs. She suspected from the lack of ornamentation it was probably another servant staircase, but she took the stairs down, the stone walls cool, the stairwell quite chilly. Pushing open a door, she discovered she was back on the ground floor, in an elegant corridor with higher ceilings, modern light fixtures, and large framed landscapes on the wall.

Ella paused before one, realizing it was a picture of Langley Park but from hundreds of years ago. The house itself had the same shape as it did now, but the outside was different, with fountains and formal gardens. There weren't many trees, at least not from this angle. It fascinated her to see how the house had evolved over the centuries.

"There you are," Baird's voice sounded from behind her. "Mrs. Booth thought we'd lost you."

Ella jumped, and then laughed, startled. "I've had an adventure," she said. "What an incredible house."

"It is."

"I take it this is the old wing, at least upstairs."

"Yes. Right around the corner is the original hall."

"I haven't made it that far. I went up the new staircase but turned left instead of right, as I'd go to Cara's room. There are so many rooms and so many hallways and staircases."

"It's a remarkable house. But I wouldn't want to be responsible for it. The maintenance never ends."

"Even on a normal house." Ella gestured to the painting she was standing in front of. "Where are the trees here? The parkland? Or has the artist just left it out?"

"There was a period of time when the trees weren't wanted. Like on many old estates, the woods were cleared to better show off the house, as well. Intricate gardens were in, natural landscapes were out."

"But the house looks so naked here."

"And yet it's more imposing, isn't it? You can also appreciate the new elegant Georgian exterior, emphasizing symmetry and classical lines."

His tone was slightly mocking, and she knew he was teasing her. "I think I prefer the Elizabethan design over the pretty Georgian era."

"As do I."

Ella flashed him a smile. "Be careful. We might end up thinking we can get along, and then where will the fun be in that?"

"You prefer a little excitement," he said, his gaze holding hers.

Just like that her heart fluttered, her traitorous pulse quickening. No, she thought, she preferred him, especially when they had fun together, and it had been a fun afternoon. Baird hadn't just survived all two hours in the kitchen, he'd known how to measure and stir things while telling amusing stories and doing wonderful accents and impersonations. He had the aunts and Mrs. Johnson howling with laughter, and Dorothy was quick to laugh, but not Emma.

"You had mad skills with the kitchen timer," she said. "We burned nothing, which pleased Emma greatly."

Baird shrugged modestly. "I'm glad I was able to impress you. It required a tremendous amount of concentration, and dexterity, getting that little dial around and then set to the right time. I would have preferred using the time on my phone, but as you heard, Emma didn't trust it."

"And it's cheating," Ella added. "There's no place for fancy technology in traditional baking."

"I think you've been listening to Emma too much."

She grinned. "You're good with them, all of them. Older ladies like you."

"I have an Aunt Kate I practice on. I've learned I have to smile a lot, agree with everything if possible, and let them think every good idea is theirs."

"I could be wrong," Ella said, still smiling, liking this Baird very much, "but that sounds like a winning combination for women of all ages. I would love to be told I'm right—every time. Why don't you do that with me?"

"Because you're not a frail senior citizen, and I can't afford to give you that much power. As it is, you're hard to manage."

"What a lovely thing to say." Ella laughed. "You are truly a silver-tongued devil."

They exited the hall and made their way back to the formal entrance, and then down the corridor to the kitchen and mudroom. Ella popped back into the kitchen and snuck a shortbread from the tin on the counter, handed it to Baird and then took one for herself.

As they left the house, they collected their coats and headed back to the cottage.

"I spoke with Alec," Baird said, "just before I found you. He's called everyone he needed to speak to and is now trying to put things in order so he can come home."

"That's good. When will he be back?"

"He's thinking he should be here in the morning."

"Does Cara know?"

"They spoke earlier today, but he's left his return a little vague in case he can't make it in the morning. He doesn't want to disappoint her but did want me to thank you for everything you're doing to entertain her and keep her from worrying. He said she loves having you here and she's so glad you can celebrate Christmas Sherbourne style."

"I love being here with her, and all of Alec's family. Mrs. Booth and Mrs. Johnson feel like Alec's family, too. I do feel rather guilty that they're both here for the holidays, though. I could probably manage more cooking if they need time off."

"Normally, Mrs. Booth would be gone, but with Cara's pregnancy she didn't feel right leaving, and Mrs. Johnson prefers to be here for Christmas and then chooses to take some time off in January once Mrs. Booth is back. This year is different from previous years, but everyone is so excited about the babies no one wants to leave."

"Cara is lucky to be surrounded by such good people. I wasn't sure what to expect, but they take very good care of her, and it's reassuring to know that she has so much support."

They walked in silence until the cottage came into view. A wisp of smoke rose from the stone chimney. "The staff loves Alec, and they know how much Cara loves Alec, and they're grateful. She's brought him to life."

They reached the cottage and Baird went straight to the fire to stoke it and add another log. Ella hung up her coat, eased off her shoes and went to a chair near the fire to get warm. "Do you see a difference in him?" she asked.

"Absolutely. He's a different man." Baird straightened and put the poker back. "There was no Christmas before, no family coming over. He hid away in that vast house, only coming home because he had to say a few words at the annual house tour. He hated the tour, too, hated people trooping through the place but now he's proud to show it off, because it's not just an old family place, but the home where he and Cara will raise their family."

"Does he talk about the babies much? What does he think about becoming a dad ... to twins?"

"I think he's in shock, but it's a good shock. There's joy and fear, but also a determination to protect her from stress and keep her safe."

Ella thought for a moment. "His news will upset her, when he shares it with her, especially if its someone Alec trusted."

Baird's jaw tightened, his expression hardening. "I hope the police find him."

"He'd be arrested, wouldn't he?"

"Yes, and with any luck, put away for a very long time."

❄

ELLA WALKED TO the house for dinner with Cara, shivering a little as temperatures were dropping and it was getting colder, cold enough that Ella suspected any rain in the forecast would turn to snow. She wouldn't mind a little snow, provided they didn't get snowed in like Cara and Alec did last year. They'd had a huge storm and had been trapped for days.

Leaving her coat and warm boots in the mudroom, Ella gave pets and scratches to the three dogs who came to see her and then continued up the stairs. But once Ella joined Cara in the bedroom, Cara was distracted and frustrated that the gifts she'd ordered hadn't arrived.

"They should have been here. They were supposed to have been here days ago," Cara said, studying delivery information on her phone. "The delivery date has now been pushed to January fifth. How does that work?"

"I already told you I'd go shopping for you," Ella answered, plopping down on the bed next to her sister. "Don't be upset. We have a plan."

"Yes, but I was hoping a couple more gifts would arrive and you might only have to buy one thing instead of four things."

"I have no plans for tomorrow. Surely, I can buy four gifts in one eight-hour day."

Cara reluctantly smiled. "I hate it when you're all practical and reasonable. Makes me feel extra unreasonable."

"Listen, I'd be bonkers if I'd spent almost two weeks up

here! Goodness, Cara, I only come for brief visits and get restless to move. I don't know how you've handled it as well as you have."

"It'll be easier when Alec is back. I just miss him."

"I know. He's going to be home soon, too, so I think we need a proper girls' night in tonight. It might be our last chance. I suggest lots of snacks and Christmas movies. What do you think?

"What about Baird? What's he doing?"

"I don't know. He might be having dinner with the senior crowd."

"Should we invite him to join us?"

Ella tossed a pillow at her sister. "No. He's not a girl."

Cara laughed and tossed the pillow right back. "Are you sure?"

"Pretty sure. I mean, he's big for a girl, not just in height, but those shoulders ... not feminine in any way."

Cara leaned forward. "Something happened between you two at the wedding, didn't it? I was sure you hooked up, but Alec said no way, never. Baird doesn't do casual hookups. He's not that kind of guy."

Ella shifted her arm to better block her sister's smiling face. "Someday when this is all over you can tell your husband that you were right, and he was wrong. Because Baird does do casual hookups."

"Where? When? Who's room?"

"No, not like that. It was during the reception, down by

the boathouse. We just kissed. A lot."

"A good kiss? Or a bad kiss?"

Ella flopped onto her back and put an arm across her eyes. "Best kiss of my life."

Cara said nothing and Ella's heart thudded hard. "And then he left early the next morning," Ella added softly.

"Did you know he was leaving early?"

"No. But I knew right away he regretted kissing me."

Cara gently combed her fingers through Ella's hair. "How?"

"He told me. I'm standing there, all warm and mushy and stupidly happy, and he announces in that gorgeous accent, that it was a mistake. It shouldn't have happened."

"Why?"

Ella shook her head. "He wasn't free. He was in a relationship with someone."

"No. That's not so. He and Fiona had broken up at the beginning of the summer. Originally, she was supposed to come to the wedding with him, but he told us in July that he would be going on his own."

Ella shouldn't ask about Fiona. She shouldn't care about Baird's past, but her curiosity was too strong. She removed her arm and looked up at Cara. "Who is Fiona?"

"His girlfriend. They'd been together for years. Alec doesn't know why they broke up. Baird never said, but Alec was pretty sure they were going to marry. They were very committed, very serious." Cara's hand stilled, her palm on

Ella's forehead. "But the breakup was two months before the wedding. Can't imagine why Baird wasn't free."

"I don't know. It doesn't matter," Ella said, soothed by Cara's touch. "We're doing our best to navigate a tricky past so that we can keep the drama down around you and Alec. We're not children. There's no need for us to have friction or tension."

"That's very mature of you." Cara leaned over Ella and smiled into her eyes. "My little sister is growing up so fast!"

Ella laughed and rolled into a sitting position. "And you're going to be a mom!

A knock sounded on the door and Cara called to come in. Mrs. Johnson entered the with a tray laden with soup and sandwiches, along with a plate of cookies and sweets. "Everyone downstairs has been fed, and I'm going to be going soon, but thought you girls might need something to snack on while you plot to take over the world."

The cook positioned the tray on the foot of the bed. "Is there anything I can do before I go?"

Cara happily eyed the tray. "This is perfect, Mrs. Johnson You always know exactly what I'm craving."

"Alright then. Sleep well and I'll see you in the morning."

"Good night," Cara said. "And thank you so much."

There was a chorus of goodnights and after the door closed behind the cook, Cara reached for the television's remote control. "Do you want a classic Christmas movie, or should we look for a romance?"

"Not a romance," Ella said, making a face. "I can do anything but that."

"Okay, let's see what we can find then."

Ella focused on a quarter sandwich while Cara scrolled through the channels, and then paused on the 2019 version of *Little Women* starring Emma Watson and Florence Pugh.

"What about this one?" Cara asked. "Or does being a Louisa May Alcott expert ruin the movies for you?"

"I haven't seen it since it came out in the theater. Would love to watch it again."

"You were exasperated by it the first time," Cara reminded her. "I don't want you to get exasperated tonight."

"I won't. I'm prepared for disappointment."

Cara laughed and pressed start on the movie before positioning pillows so they could sit side by side against the headboard. As the music swelled Cara smiled happily at Ella. "This is fun."

Ella smiled back. "It's exactly what I hoped we'd do."

BAIRD HAD HIS work spread around him on the cottage table, files for clients, cases coming up, depositions to be reviewed. There was never a slow season in his field. If anything, the holidays only heightened discord, and every January there was an uptick in cases. More divorces, more acrimonious settlements, more custody battles. He used to find the sheer number of clients, along with their unhappiness, depressing. Now, he merely saw it was a fact of life, and a job he was paid well to do. It was a lucrative profession if you could keep the stories of betrayal and hostility from getting under your skin.

For the most part, Baird was good at separating work and his home life. He didn't take work home, and he never discussed his clients or cases.

But he'd be lying if his work hadn't influenced him. Damaged was the word Fiona liked to use during their last month together. Practicing family law had damaged him, making him cynical, and bitter, unable to love.

Yes, he'd become cynical, but he could still love. He could feel. He desired. He didn't desire marriage, though. He wasn't interested in having children. It wasn't a game, or a ploy; it wasn't his attempt to keep women away. He just knew himself, and knew he'd be happier not marrying.

He'd always thought Fiona felt that way. They'd met each other when she was in med school, and he was in law school. They were both ambitious and shared similar values, and over the years as their friendship grew, they grew closer, until one day they shifted from friends to lovers.

Because they both worked long hours, they understood the demands of each other's career. While Fiona was locked down at the hospital as a surgeon, his law practice had him traveling all over the world. He wasn't interested in other women. Fiona was beautiful and brilliant, and the ideal companion. She never asked for too much, and he never expected anything from her—expectations always lead to disappointment and conflict. It worked for them. They were happy.

Until the day Fiona asked about the future, their future, and how he saw it playing out.

Playing out? The question surprised Baird. What was wrong with things as they were? They were a popular power couple in Edinburgh, which was close to where Fiona was from. He hadn't minded moving from Glasgow. He hadn't objected to sharing her place—how could he—it was a gorgeous three-bedroom flat with enormous bay windows and lots of natural light, a necessity in a city like Edinburgh.

Who knew that Fiona's innocent question would unravel everything? But it did, quickly. Fiona felt the pressure of her ticking biological clock. She, who'd never expressed desire for children, now longed for them. Wanted them. And begged Baird to start a family with her.

But Baird had no plans to marry. He had no desire to be a father. He thought Fiona understood that. He thought he and Fiona were both happy being childless. They were partners, even without the piece of paper. It was a good life, a fulfilling life. They had each other and work they loved. What more could one want?

Apparently, a great deal.

Fiona wanted to be a mother. She wanted to marry. She

didn't know why she couldn't be a surgeon, Baird's wife, and mother to his children. They were happy together, good together, weren't they?

Baird tried to explain his position. If things were good, why change anything?

If they were happy, why not continue as they were?

But Fiona was no longer happy. She didn't shout or throw things, rather she retreated somewhere inside of herself, her eyes enormous with grief and pain. She focused on the fact that he wouldn't marry *her*, that he wouldn't have children with *her*, not caring that he didn't want to marry anyone, or have children with anyone. Couldn't she see that it wasn't personal? Couldn't she see that nothing had changed?

But it had.

As the months warmed, spring creeping closer to summer, work consumed them, but the ties that had always been there between them were unraveling, the trust broken.

In late May, they agreed to take a break. Baird, who'd bought a building a mile away, would move into one of the flats which was becoming available June first. Living apart would give them time and space, hopefully allowing them to come to a consensus.

Fiona agreed. Yes, to time and space. Maybe being apart would make Baird remember what he'd loved about her.

But the time apart didn't heal, and Fiona realized Baird would never change his mind, and she wasn't going to give up her dreams just to make him happy. Just like that, four years with Fiona was over.

Baird missed her. You didn't just stop loving someone overnight. But he was also relieved. He couldn't give Fiona what she wanted. It was better this way. She could meet someone new, someone who would want a family, and he could focus again on work.

It was in this reflective mindset that Baird arrived in Seattle for the wedding. It had been a revelation traveling by ferry, so much beauty in the Puget Sound, so much warmth and sunshine.

Baird had needed this trip, needed to get away. It felt good to be somewhere new. For the first time in months he could breathe, relax. Arriving at the resort, he checked into his room, a stunning suite with an equally stunning view of the water and the harbor, then showered and dressed for the welcome cocktail party. With fifteen minutes before the party began, he pushed open his sliding glass door and stepped out onto his balcony, savoring the scent of pine and golden rays of light.

That's when he saw her, an angelic vision with long red hair, dressed in the palest shade of blue, her long full skirt swirling around her legs.

Her profile was so much like Cara's—her build was so much like Cara's—he knew immediately who she was. Ella, the younger sister, the brilliant scholar who graduated from high school at sixteen, and was flying through graduate school, soon to be a full-fledged professor in her own right.

Baird watched her, intrigued. He'd heard a lot about her. And for the first time in months, he didn't feel dead.

Watching her greet two guests, affectionately hugging first the wife and then the husband, Baird knew Ella was different, special. His body knew it, too, tightening with awareness, hardening with desire. He couldn't remember the last time he'd felt such intense desire. He didn't even know Ella yet, but she'd already changed his world, knocking him off balance, taking his breath away.

He couldn't wait to meet her and yet he could.

He wasn't ready for someone like Ella, wasn't ready to want anyone, wasn't ready to live again.

And yet as the breeze caught her long hair and pale blue skirt, she reminded him of the tiny ballerina in his sister Maisie's jewelry box, the ballerina so delicate and beautiful in its tiny white tutu it almost hurt to watch her twirl, one pirouette after another.

He felt that same bittersweet awe now. Ella was glorious and impossibly alive. She was not of this world, and if he wasn't careful, she would change everything.

Absolutely everything.

And she did.

ELLA HAD FALLEN asleep with Cara watching one movie after

the other. She only woke when the TV turned off and she opened her eyes to discover Alec there, setting his luggage down by the door.

He put a finger to his lips. "Go back to sleep. I'll crash in the next room."

Ella shook her head and climbed from the bed.

Yawning, she pulled Alec out of the room and into the dimly lit hallway. "I'm not taking your bed. Cara will be so happy to wake up and find you there. Let me just get my shoes and I'll let myself out."

"Where are you going?"

"The cottage. I'm staying—" She broke off, frowning. Did Alec know she and Baird were sharing the cottage? "I'm staying at the cottage where Cara stayed last Christmas."

"But isn't Baird staying there?"

"Yes. I wish I could say it's an interesting story but it's not. We're both very stubborn, and we both thought we should have it, so there we are." She smiled at her brother-in-law, genuinely happy to see him. "I'm good to walk back so let me grab my shoes and phone and I'll see you in the morning."

"I'm not letting you walk back by yourself. Get your things and I'll take you."

Ella knew better to argue, and in the mudroom, she retrieved her coat, slid her arms into the jacket and zipped it up. Alec opened the door and she gasped at the gust of wind.

"Wow. That's cold," she said.

"The weather is changing."

"Does that mean snow for Christmas?" she asked hopefully as he held the passenger door open for her.

"Probably not for Christmas, but maybe for New Year's."

"Too bad."

He smiled faintly. "You're just as bad as your sister."

And suddenly Ella remembered how awful Alec's past few days had been, and how heartsick and guilty he must have felt calling all those clients, letting them know the terrible news.

She wrapped her arms around him and gave him a fierce hug. "It's good to see you," she said. "I hope you know how much I love you."

For a second, Alec was still, and then he hugged her back. "Thank you," he said gruffly.

She let him go and climbed into the car, glad he couldn't see she was blinking back tears. This was so not the Christmas she'd expected, but maybe it was better. She was here to help, here available, to do anything and everything, whether it was clear the table or give hugs. Sometimes one just needed to be surrounded by love.

It was a very quick drive to the cottage. Ella thanked Alec and slipped from the car after he'd pulled up in front of the cottage door.

Entering the dark cottage, Ella was grateful Baird had left a light on near the stairs. She hung up her coat, eased off her shoes and tiptoed up the steep staircase, avoiding the steps that tended to creak. The last thing she wanted to do was wake him. But just as she was reaching for her doorknob, Baird's door opened.

"Who drove you here?" Baird asked from the shadows enveloping his room.

She couldn't see him well, but he appeared to be wrapped in some kind of enormous robe, reminding her of a Viking on a midwinter's night. Except he wasn't a Viking, he was a Celt.

"Alec did," she said. "He's just returned home."

"Cara must be glad."

"Cara was fast asleep when we left. But yes, she'll be so happy to see Alec when she wakes up."

"How did he seem?" Baird asked.

"Good. Tired. But typically Alec, impossibly polite."

"I'm glad he's back."

Ella reached for her doorknob. "Thank you for leaving the light on for me."

"Of course."

"I am sorry I woke you, though."

"I wasn't asleep. I'd stayed up in case you needed someone to walk you back."

A hot wash of emotion flooded Ella, making the air bottle in her lungs. "If I'd known, I would have texted you—"

"It's okay. I'm glad you had a nice night with Cara."

"Me, too."

Chapter Six

Alec and Cara were seated in the lovely sunlit breakfast room when Ella walked up to the house the next morning. The aunts were there as well, but Uncle Frederick was having a lazy morning, and Mrs. Johnson had taken tea and toast to him in his room.

"I hope he's feeling okay," Ella said, grateful to see Mrs. Johnson with the coffee pot.

"He's slowing down," Emma said, "and likes his morning routine, but I think he's otherwise quite well."

Ella glanced at Alec and Cara who were seated next to each other. Cara was holding Alec's hand and Ella knew from her sister's expression that Alec had shared his news with her about the employee stealing funds. Cara wasn't weepy, but her expression was somber.

Neither of the aunts mentioned anything about the calls they'd received or asked about London or Langley Investments. Breakfast proceeded as if everything was normal, except somewhat quieter with less frivolous chatter.

Baird arrived as the plates were being cleared. He'd gone for a run, taking Milo and Albert with him, and had showered and changed before joining them. Mrs. Johnson asked if she could make him some eggs, but he said he'd already had something at the cottage, but he wouldn't turn down coffee.

With coffees refreshed, and sunlight shining through the tall windows, Cara looked at Alec and gave him a small smile. "What do you think about sharing our news?" she asked him. "I know we were going to wait until Christmas Eve, but it might be a good time now."

"You don't want to wait until Uncle Frederick is here?" Alec answered.

"You and I could go to his room after and share the news with him. It might make him feel special."

Alec glanced toward Emma and Dorothy. "Although, I suspect *they* suspect something. What with all the carrying you up and down the stairs."

Ella couldn't hide her smile. "Cara's ankle is healing nicely. While you were gone, Baird has been very conscientious about keeping her off her feet or at least as much as she will allow."

"We think we know," Dorothy said. "Emma and I have discussed it, but we didn't want to get our hopes up."

"Let's hear what you think our news is," Alec said, lifting Cara's hand to his lips and pressing a kiss to the back of her fingers.

Emma hesitated as she carefully replaced her cup in the saucer. "We are hoping that there will soon be a new generation of Sherbournes." She looked at Alec and Cara. "That would be truly wonderful news."

Cara blushed, her happiness evident. "You tell them, sweetheart. I think since you had to give them bad news two days ago, it should be you that gives them good news now."

"We are expecting," he said, voice pitched low. "With a May due date."

Dorothy clapped her hands. "I knew it, I knew it. I'm so glad to hear this."

"I don't suppose you know what you're having?" Emma asked. "Or have you found out? I'm not sure when you can find out."

Cara shook her head. "We haven't found out. But during one of the early ultrasounds, we had a surprise." She paused for dramatic effect. "We're not having just one baby. There are two."

"Twins?" Dorothy gasped.

"Fraternal twins," Alec clarified. "So, there could be two boys, two girls, one of each. We don't know. But everything looks healthy. Cara just needs to not overexert herself, give the babies a chance to mature, and everything should be okay."

"Were things not okay, Alec?" Dorothy asked.

"There were some challenges early on," he answered. "There was a period of time where we were told she could lose one or both. Her doctor, a leading obstetrician, with a lot of experience with multiples, recommended Cara spend as much time off of her feet as possible. And she's done that." He looked at everyone gathered at the table. "Now we just have to keep her quietly entertained until the doctor gives the all clear."

"With that in mind, Ella has promised to take care of some of my last-minute Christmas shopping," Cara said.

"I have some things I'd like to buy, too, so this is perfect," Ella answered, finishing her coffee and folding her napkin and placing it next to her plate.

"I don't suppose you could drive Ella to town, Baird?" Cara asked hopefully. "I know it's going to be crowded, and parking might be a nightmare, but I always think having a car to put packages in makes shopping, easier."

"Oh, count me in. I'd love to go Christmas shopping," Baird answered, a playful light in his warm brown eyes. "Especially on the busiest shopping day of the year."

Everyone laughed and Cara promised to send Ella her shopping list. Ella and Baird returned to the cottage to get ready for their day out. Ella changed into warmer clothes and shoes that would be warm, and good for walking. Dressed, she drew her hair into a ponytail and slicked on some lipstick, before grabbing an additional sweater from the foot of her bed and heading downstairs.

Baird was outside at the car already, cleaning off the windshield and knocking away fallen leaves.

He looked so industrious buffing off his windshield, making her think of a warrior preparing his sword for battle, that she laughed out loud.

He glanced up and caught her smile. "What are you giggling about now?"

"You're doing an excellent job cleaning the glass. I'm impressed."

"I don't think that was why you were laughing."

"Okay, I was actually picturing you in a kilt cleaning your sword, but I didn't want to make you uncomfortable."

"I do have a kilt, but sadly, no sword."

"Every warrior should have a sword."

"Or a bow and arrow."

"Would you have preferred a bow and arrow?" she asked, climbing into the passenger seat after he'd opened the door for her.

"Why does it have to be one or the other?" he answered, closing the door firmly behind her.

Ella just smiled, and she kept smiling because she was looking forward to spending the morning with Baird, not at the house, not with all the relatives, but just being out and doing something different, and feeling free.

As Baird started the car, Ella glanced at Cara's list. Cara wanted a silvery blue cardigan for Dorothy, a cashmere shawl in brown and gold tones for Emma, and for Uncle Frederick dark brown driving gloves, fur lined if possible. Cara had written down sizes, with the note that UK sizes were different than US sizes. Ella noticed that Cara hadn't put anything down for Alec, but maybe that was because she'd already purchased something for him before being put on bedrest.

Christmas shopping in an English village was nothing like shopping at home with the American big malls and chain retailers. The shops in Bakewell were small and each unique. The town itself was teeming with people and cars. Everything had been decorated and exuded so much holiday spirit that Ella was practically bouncing in her seat, eager to be outside and part of the festive atmosphere.

Cars were clogging the narrow roads, everyone competing for a parking spot, but Baird found one when Ella was sure they'd never get lucky. He parked in the tiny spot with enviable ease and then out of the car, he took Ella's arm and navigated the crowded streets as if he was an intrepid New Yorker.

"I can tell you've lived in big cities," Ella said, as he straight armed a boy who nearly ran into her. "You know how to clear a path."

"It helps when you're bigger than most," he answered, keeping her close to his side.

Ella liked how protective he was and felt warm and wonderfully safe with her hand in his arm, and his big frame sheltering her from pedestrians too busy talking and eating to realize their strollers and shopping baskets were bumping into everyone else.

They crossed the street, and ahead a trio of musicians played on one corner while a magician performed on another, hoping to earn a few coins. Bakewell looked like something from a movie with all the wreaths on doors and windows, and the greenery and candles in other shop windows. One shop had a particularly long line, and Ella was fascinated by the sign. *The Original Bakewell Tart.* She didn't know what a Bakewell tart was, but it sounded delicious and, from the line forming out the door and onto the street, it was certainly popular.

"Have you ever had one?" she asked Baird who had assigned himself the job of carrying packages once she'd begun to make purchases.

"I have, but not here. Mrs. Johnson makes an excellent Bakewell tart, and I've only had hers."

Baird had used his phone to look up clothing stores in Bakewell, and they went from one to another with Ella popping inside each store to see if they had carried cardigans or women's shawls. There were some lovely woven goods in the second, but nothing like the items on Cara's shopping list. Ella left the shop and went outside to where Baird was waiting for her, leaning against the building, his big shoulder resting on weathered stone. In his vintage leather coat, and dark navy plaid scarf carelessly tied around his throat, he was drawing admiring looks from women walking by. She didn't blame them. She was rather smitten, too.

"Well?" he asked, straightening.

She shook her head. "Nothing. They did have a pretty cardigan in a lovely pink color, but I don't think that's what Cara is wanting. I think we have to keep looking."

"There are two more shops on the other side of town.

We'll go there now and if we can't find what you need, we'll head to the next town. It you don't mind a drive, we could always just go straight to Sheffield. They've have everything there. It's a proper city."

"You mean a big city?"

"Half a million, so not big by American standards."

"I do prefer the villages though. I'd rather try a few other small towns first if we could."

"I'd good with that," Baird said, leading the way down the street and around the corner. They walked several blocks and then came to a clothing store, with another across the street. "They might have the men's driving gloves in that one." Baird gestured to the shop across the street. "I'll see if they carry any and you check that shop and maybe one of us will get lucky."

Baird found a pair of dark brown leather driving gloves, beautifully lined, and paid for them, assuring Ella that she could give him Cara's money later.

Ella didn't find the sweater or shawl Cara wanted, and with the gloves tucked into Baird's coat pocket, they headed back to the car to try Chesterfield, which was only eleven miles away, and while not a big city, was bigger than the local villages and would offer more stores and shops.

Ella was immediately charmed by Chesterfield, another market town with a two-thousand-year-old history, dating back to its founding as a Roman fort. Thanks to the development of roads, Chesterfield became a prosperous market town during the Middle Ages and the city still boasted an impressive historic square with ancient churches and period buildings anchoring the sides. A towering Christmas tree dominated the center and shoppers and carolers filled the square.

It took almost an hour, but Ella found a shawl she thought Cara would approve of and a lovely soft cardigan in silver gray which would be a perfect foil for Dorothy's silver white hair.

They had a break for a light snack to keep their energy up, but now with the shopping done, and twilight several hours away, Baird suggested they stop by Bolsover Castle to have a look, if Ella liked castles.

"How can one not like castles?" she asked, returning to Baird's car with him.

"I don't know, but you Americans are a strange lot."

"Ha!"

He laughed. "I'm only teasing you. I was going to drag you to Bolsover whether you wanted to go or not."

It was a fifteen-minute drive to Bolsover, and even though it was just a day before Christmas Eve, the parking lot was full, and there were dozens of families coming and going, their children adorably dressed in their holiday finest.

"I wonder if Father Christmas is here," Baird said, parking.

"Or maybe a holiday concert?" she asked, charmed by a little girl in a cherry-red coat with matching ribbon in her hair.

"Perhaps," he agreed.

But as they approached the ticket booth, they saw the sign that Festive Stories with Father Christmas had sold out, and Father Christmas would return next year.

"You were right," Ella said. "Santa is here."

The woman selling tickets said that admission was fourteen pounds each, and even though Father Christmas was booked for the day, the Victorian carolers were walking the castle grounds and would be performing for the next hour.

Ella took a pamphlet on the history of Bolsover, reading the castle's history aloud to Baird, sharing that it dated back to 1068 but was abandoned in the 1300s. Three hundred years later a Sir Charles Cavendish rebuilt part of the ruins into a smaller castle, making it his principal seat, and for the next thousand years it went like that—construction, destruction, construction, disrepair. By the early 1920s, the castle was little more than romantic ruins, the massive limestone bedrock showing huge cracks which threatened the remaining castle's stability. If it wasn't for the British Ministry of Works stepping in at the end of WWII, the castle wouldn't be open to the public today.

Ella closed the pamphlet. "That's a lot of history. I always think the 1700s are old."

"It is. Just not if you're a castle or a Roman fort."

She pocketed the pamphlet and kept her hands inside her coat, wanting to warm them. "I thought Alec looked good this morning. Better than I expected."

"I'm glad he's back home. It's where he needs to be now." Baird was about to add something when suddenly the Victorian carolers were upon them, singing "The Holly and the Ivy."

The castle walls created outstanding acoustics. Other castle visitors circled around, everyone hushed and savoring the old English carol. The carolers sang two more songs before moving on, and Ella watched them go, moved. A lump filled her throat and her heart felt tender. "That was so beautiful."

Baird glanced at her. "I'm glad you enjoyed it."

She blinked, smiling through a sheen of tears. "It feels like Christmas."

"It's almost here, isn't it?"

She nodded and he gave her a hug. "Who knew you were such a sensitive little thing," he said playfully, his tone kind and his hug was warm.

Baird's unexpected thoughtfulness made the lump in her throat just grow. She didn't even know she'd needed this—the outing, the carolers, the hug—but she did. "Thank you for bringing me here. This is my favorite day so far."

"If you like this, you must come to Edinburgh for the Military Tattoo. I take my parents and Aunt Kate every August, and it never fails to make me proud of my country and my heritage."

"What is the Military Tattoo?"

"The most splendid concert imaginable, featuring the very best military bands from all over the world, performing in the center of the castle. Unlike here, where Bolsover is outside the town, Edinburgh Castle is in the middle of the old city, rising up from Castle Rock."

"Sounds wonderful. I'd love to see it one day."

"You'd like Edinburgh. But I suggest visiting the first time in summer. The winter can be harsh."

Ella was intrigued. "Do you have a house or an apartment? Do you live alone or have a roommate?"

"No roommate," he said as they turned at the turret and began the walk back. "I have a building in the old part of town and rent out the two lower floors—one is a two-bedroom apartment and the other is a three bedroom. I live on the top floor, the third floor. It's well situated, a corner building, with huge windows in each of the front living rooms. The building needed extensive repairs when I first bought it, but if it weren't in such poor shape, I probably couldn't have afforded it."

"Does your apartment have a garden or balcony?"

"No. But there are city parks in every direction should I crave some outdoor space."

As they emerged from the tower and out into the center quad, a bell rang, alerting them that the castle would be closing soon.

"It's going to be dark soon," Ella said. "I can't believe how quickly the day went."

"We haven't even had a proper meal," Baird said, pushing open the gate, allowing Ella to exit before he followed.

"We could eat when we return to Langley Park as we're only a half hour away, or we could stop somewhere for a bite on the way. What would you prefer?"

"I'd love to stop at a pub or restaurant. I'm up for experiencing everything I can while I'm here."

BAIRD HAD ENJOYED the day. He wasn't even going to pretend that it had been a bother taking Ella shopping. While he wasn't a fan of crowds, and every place they went was ridiculously crowded, he couldn't think of anyone he'd rather navigate crowds with.

Ella made him smile. She also frustrated him, making him want things he shouldn't want, not with her, Alec's sister-in-law.

But every time he looked at her, at that full upper lip and her very full bottom lip, he remembered kissing her, remembered how he'd come alive, hungry, voracious.

He still wanted her. He still fought the attraction but now suppressed it knowing just how explosive it was between them, and how quickly desire consumed them. The sheer heat in their kiss, in that wild desperate hunger, blew him away. He'd never experienced anything like that, he'd never felt need that was so elemental and consuming. It had shocked him. Unnerved him.

Baird, who valued logic and reason, couldn't make sense

of the passion. He wasn't a man who physically needed anyone, or anything. Until Ella.

He didn't like it, though. He liked her, but not the intense emotions. They didn't fit in his world. They didn't line up with his values. He liked his life ordered. He was a man who kept to his rules. There was no reason to take risks, never mind lose control.

In the car, Baird called one of his and Alec's favorite restaurants in Bakewell to see if they had any reservations available for two that evening."

"We've just had a cancellation for half six," the host said. "Can you make that?"

"We can."

"We'll only be able to hold the table for ten minutes," the host added.

"No problem. We'll be there."

They made it back to Bakewell with five minutes to spare. Parking at the restaurant was far easier than it had been earlier today. He went around to open the door for Ella who gave him such a dazzling smile that for a moment he forgot why he couldn't have her, and then as she stepped out, putting her hand in his, he felt the spark between them, that stunning electric awareness he'd never felt with anyone else, and knew why he had to keep her at arm's length.

This. This heat. These sparks. They weren't logical. There was nothing safe in desire. It would have been different if they'd been brought together by work, or shared values, but heat? Sex?

No. That was no basis for a real relationship.

At the restaurant, he gave his name, and they were immediately escorted to a table against the wall. A few heads turned as they walked to their table. Baird held her chair and then sat down across from her.

She leaned across the table, lips curving. "You draw attention everywhere you go," she said. "Women love you."

He looked at her, bemused. "What women?"

"The women who watch you with hungry eyes." She grinned. "They look as if they're starving, Baird. How can you not notice?"

"You're mistaken. Heads turn because of you," he answered. "You're stunning."

SHE LOVED THE way he said stunning, in his gorgeous accent, the syllables rolling off his tongue. "I think you have it wrong, but I'm too happy to be here to argue with you. Perhaps tomorrow we can become adversaries again."

"And why should we become adversaries? I'd rather be on good terms with you."

She couldn't help smiling at him. "You've lost that stern look, Baird MacLauren. You almost look … kind."

"I am kind." His lips curved faintly. "Sometimes."

"Can I ask you something? About you know. August."

His expression turned wary. "I thought you decided it was best that we avoided all mentions and conversation of that particular event."

"I did. And we probably shouldn't discuss, but I have this little voice in my head, and it won't be quiet, and it won't leave me alone."

"That sounds very serious."

"It is. Which is why I would like a serious answer from you."

"I'll do my best, Eloise."

She grimaced. "Now you just want to fight."

"I don't. I promise. What is your question?"

Ella's courage nearly deserted her. She wasn't sure why she thought this would be good dinner table conversation.

"Come on," he urged. "Out with it. You can't leave me hanging. I'm anticipating something big."

"Okay. Here it is." She leaned toward him a little and dropped her voice. "If we kissed now, what do you think would happen?"

Baird just stared at her, his gold eyes narrowing, a tiny muscle pulling in his cheek.

"I'm not being provocative," she hastened to add. "I genuinely want to know. Would the kiss still be all sparky and hot, or would we realize it was just the setting, what with the moonlight and all."

His gaze skimmed her face, sweeping over her eyes, her cheeks, her mouth until his attention was focused only there, on her lips.

He hadn't even said a word and yet her mouth began to pulse, hot, sensitive, so sensitive.

"What makes you ask?" he said at length, his voice pitched so low that it rumbled through her, making her feel as if there was no space between them. He might as well have his hands in her hair, tipping her head back to claim her mouth, her lips, her tongue.

She swallowed hard. "Because I thought if... if... the magic was gone, we'd be safe. You know, you and me together. I thought maybe without the heat we could be friends. Good friends."

"Let me have your hand," he said, extending his to her.

She looked down at his open palm, his hand large, his fingers strong. She could see each of the lines across his palm, the smaller lines on his fingers. Nervous, she hesitated and then she carefully put her palm on his, flat against his, palm to palm, skin to skin. His hand was warm, steady. For a moment, nothing happened. For a moment, she thought she was free.

And then he slowly slid his palm beneath hers, slipping it across her own and it was like striking a match. Heat flared and exquisite sensation streaked through her, the pleasure so intense it made her dizzy.

She jerked her head up and looked into his eyes. His gold eyes smoldered. His firm lips pressed together and yet she could feel them, how they'd touched her in August. On her mouth, on her neck, on the pulse just below her ear.

Heart racing, Ella pulled her hand back, burying it in her lap.

"Well?" he drawled. "Are we safe?"

"Sure," Ella lied, voice quavering as she reached for her menu. "Perfectly safe. How about you?"

"Probably as safe as you."

CHAPTER SEVEN

SHE LOVED FIRE, Baird thought, forcing himself to eat even though he wasn't hungry for food. And being Ella, she had to test the attraction. She had to make sure it was real.

It was real.

And now the heat was back, and the desire hummed, and it was not going to be easy to just pretend to be friends when he wanted her. But Baird was nothing if not competitive, and if she wanted to eat dinner as if nothing had happened, then he'd play the game, bite for bite.

But as dinner progressed, she began struggling with her pretense, taking longer to chew, longer to swallow, longer to lift her fork to her mouth. Ever since the food arrived, they'd been quiet, but she'd look at him every now and then, a question in her eyes, searching his, looking for something. He wondered if she even knew what she was looking for.

She was looking at him now, her eyes like the North Sea, a deep blue with a hint of green. He lifted a brow, hoping to encourage her.

"What do you think they're having for dinner at Langley

Park?" she asked, voice unsteady.

He fought an urge to laugh. That wasn't what was on her mind, but he'd give her points for trying. "I can't imagine it's steak frites," he said, which is what they were both having. Who knew steak frites was Ella's favorite meal? It had always been one of his.

"Mrs. Johnson is a good cook, though."

"Yes," he agreed gravely trying to match her tone.

What he wanted to do was laugh and pull her out of her chair and onto his lap and kiss her the way she wanted to be kissed. He could feel the yearning in her. Whatever string bound them, it was tight, pulling them in, pulling them so close that every time she took a breath, he could feel it.

Finally, he put down his fork, unwilling to continue the game all dinner. "So, what do we do now? Do we go back to the cottage and start what we began last summer?"

Her eyes widened and her lips parted but no sound came out.

"Or do we just keep pretending nothing is there and we're both happy and fine," he added. "Would love to know what we're supposed to do."

Ella set her fork down now and it clattered against her plate. "But we are both happy and fine." She didn't look at him as she pushed her plate away. "Aren't we?"

"If we were fifteen, sure. But we're adults. Sneaking kisses is an appetizer, it's not a meal. As a man, I'd be lying if I find it completely satisfying."

Her head lifted, her eyes briefly meeting his before just as swiftly looking away. "Did... do ... you want more?"

He shouldn't torment her, but she had it coming. She started this.

He'd only been with one woman in the past four years, and sex with Fiona was nice, and life with her had been good, but it had never felt remotely like this. "Don't you?" he countered, studying Ella so intently that she had to look up, had to gaze back, had to see just what he was feeling.

"Why didn't you marry Fiona?" Ella asked abruptly. "Cara and Alec were sure you were going to be together, always."

Nothing could have cooled his ardor like mentioning Fiona and marriage in the same sentence. "What do you know of Fiona?" he asked.

"Only that you were together a long time. You were happy together ... until you weren't."

"But isn't that the way of relationships? They work until they don't?"

"If you were that serious, if you'd been together that many years, couldn't you work through your differences?" Ella persisted. "Wasn't the relationship worth saving?"

He did not want to be drawn into this. "I couldn't give her what she wanted."

"Didn't you love her?"

He was being drawn into this. Baird smashed his irritation. "I did. But she wanted to marry, and we'd agreed years before that I wasn't going to marry, and she knew, she'd agreed. I thought we were both content, and then I discovered I was wrong. She loved me, but the need to have a family was stronger, and we agreed she'd be happier with someone who could give her what she wanted."

"That's why you broke up?" Ella whispered, stunned.

"Did you think there was something more nefarious? That one of us had done the other wrong?"

Ella gave her head a slight shake. She seemed confused and terribly sad.

"You don't need to feel bad for Fi. She's already met a wonderful doctor who loves her madly and is eager to marry her. The wedding is in February. It's happening soon."

Ella's forehead creased. "And that doesn't bother you?"

"Of course not. It's good. It's great. A relief."

"A *relief?*"

"Her clock was ticking and all that."

Ella looked away, but not before he saw disappointment in her eyes, and felt her disappointment in him. He didn't understand it. Why did she care so much about Fiona? What business was it of hers?

"You're never going to marry ... not anyone?" she persisted.

"No. Marriage is not in my future. It's not something I want."

"Not even if you met the right person?"

"If I'd wanted marriage, I would have married Fi. But I

didn't want marriage. It's as simple as that."

Baird rarely explained himself to anyone, and he didn't owe Ella an explanation, either, but her bewilderment touched him. She truly didn't understand.

"I've seen what people do to each other," he said. "I've seen too much of the ugliness that happens when a marriage sours. I've seen what it does to the children. I don't want that. I don't ever want anything like that."

"What makes you think you would have such a toxic relationship? Not every marriage ends in divorce."

"Enough do that it's not logical for me to take that next step."

"I don't believe love is logical."

"Even more reason to avoid it."

Her brow arched. "You really mean that?"

"I do."

"But you seem so … well-adjusted."

He nearly laughed. "I'd like to think I am, and just because I don't want to get married or have kids—"

"You don't want kids, either?"

"Before you ask if I don't like kids, it's not that. I love kids. I love my nieces and nephews, and I can't wait to be a godfather to the twins. I want to be in their lives. I look forward to being there for them. But no, I'm not planning on starting a family, and have no desire to put children in the middle of something that could be contentious, turning them into pawns in someone else's game for vengeance—"

"That's so harsh, Baird."

"But it's real. I see it on a daily basis. A good marriage can be wonderful. A bad marriage can be vile. I've seen those vile marriages in action. It's the last thing I'd want. It's the last thing I could accept."

"What makes you think you'd be that husband or that father?"

"A marriage is made up of two people. I can only control me, and who I want to be.

I don't get to control or make choices for my partner. Nor would I want to. But over time, people become disillusioned in their mate. They fall out of love. They feel hurt, or neglected. They realize they made a mistake. Sex isn't good. Finances are tight. The person you thought you knew supports a politician you detest. Once the disillusionment sets in, it's very difficult to recover from. Which is where I come in."

"It's a miracle anyone makes it," Ella said under her breath.

"I heard that," he said, completely serious. "And I agree."

THEY LEFT THE restaurant and instead of returning straight to the car, took a walk around Bakewell, enjoying the lights and the brightly illuminated Christmas tree in the center of town. Ella was glad to be out, moving. She couldn't stop replaying their dinner conversation over and over in her head, and the replays didn't help. The replays just made her feel worse.

"What's on your mind?" Baird asked as they walked along the riverbank.

She shook her head. "Nothing and everything." She looked up at him. "All at the same time."

He plucked a strand of hair from her eyelashes. "That's a lot."

"It is. It's too much."

"Maybe stop thinking for a bit. You don't have to have all the answers tonight. You can just relax. Be."

"Easy for you to say," she muttered.

"How so?"

"I can't think straight, not around you, Baird. Why is that?"

"I don't know, but if it's any consolation, it's mutual."

She looked up, into his eyes. "Is it?"

"Yeah."

He wasn't classically handsome and yet she thought he was the most beautiful man in the world. His eyes, his nose, his mouth. But of everything, she had a special fondness for his nose, with that bump. "How did you get that?" she asked, reaching up to lightly touch his nose.

"Broke it in a fight."

"Do you fight much?"

"Try not to."

"So, you're a peaceful man."

"Peaceful enough," Baird said, drawing her closer. "I don't start fights. I just finish them."

She felt fizzy and dizzy all at the same time. "Are you good with those fists?"

Baird lifted one hand, clenching it. "I can handle myself, and others, if need be."

"Impressive."

Baird smiled, amused. "Are you a bloodthirsty wench?"

"I do find a strong man sexy." Her face grew warm. "But please know, I'm not flirting. I'm just being truthful."

He suddenly flexed, his bicep bunching. "Have I shown you my muscles lately?"

"You have never shown me your muscles."

"What about at the wedding?"

"You were wearing the tuxedo jacket."

"A shame."

Then he kissed her, a slow, sweet melting kiss that made her sigh and lean into him. Just as quickly as the kiss began, it was over. Ella whimpered in protest.

Baird ran his thumb across her soft, sensitive lower lip. "You drive me mad, Eloise."

"Not Eloise."

"Eloise to me."

She rolled her eyes but also laughed. "You are impossible. This is impossible. I thought we were fighting the attraction."

"We are," he said solemnly. "We're not giving in."

"What was that kiss then?"

"A reminder that we must remain on guard, vigilant to threats and danger."

Ella slowly shook her head, aware that she'd already lost that war. Baird had snared her heart and she doubted he'd ever give it back.

Pulling up to the cottage a half hour later, things looked vastly different from how they'd left the cottage this morning. White fairy lights sparkled from inside the cottage. A fresh fragrant wreath hung on the front door. Ella glanced at Baird as he turned the engine off, but he seemed as surprised as she did.

"What's happened?" she asked a slight catch in her voice, surprise and confusion.

"Somebody's been here," he said.

Somebody had been there. Entering the cottage, they discovered the rustic interior had been transformed into the most charming Christmas wonderland with a lush tabletop tree covered in little lights and delicate ornaments. Fresh greenery adorned the mantle, boughs dotted with white votive candles that were all glowing. More greenery hung above the kitchen window, the greenery decorated with dried slices of oranges and lemons and charming green plaid bows.

Ella looked around and then at Baird, completely in awe. "Who did this?"

"I don't know. Your sister maybe?"

"She couldn't have done it herself."

"Maybe with Alec's then?" he answered, entering the kitchen and going to the stove where a copper pot sat on the burner. He removed the lid, and cinnamon and spice filled the air. "Mulled wine." He glanced at her. "Should we have a cup?"

"I think we must." Ella laughed. "Mulled wine, in England, by the fire. How can it get any better than this?"

"We could be having mulled wine in Scotland by the fire."

They stayed up late talking—chatting, really—about nothing and everything and with a blanket wrapped around her and the fire cracking and popping Ella felt good, relieved to have things comfortable between her and Baird again. She learned a lot that evening about Christmas in the United Kingdom, not realizing how different countries had such different customs. She hadn't known that Christmas in Scotland had been banned for hundreds of years, and baking Yule bread had been a criminal act. Christmas didn't even become a recognized holiday until the 1950s, which was why Hogmanay was such a special occasion in Scotland. Since the people couldn't celebrate Christmas, New Year's became incredibly important.

Finally, it was time to go to bed and Ella helped blow out the candles, but she lingered for a moment by the tree, not yet wanting to unplug the lights. "It was the best surprise," she said. "Can't wait to thank Alec and Cara."

In bed, Ella sent a quick text to her sister. Thank you for the most wonderful surprise. I love it all. It's absolutely magical!

Cara didn't answer, but Ella wasn't surprised. Cara was going to bed early these days and when she woke up, she'd see the text.

BAIRD WAS OUT for his early morning run, frost glittering everywhere. It was a beautiful morning, the air cold, the sky blue. There was no snow in the forecast, but the frost was just as beautiful, turning everything a glittery white.

He heard dogs barking and turned to see Otis and Milo running toward him, with Alec not far behind.

"Look at you, laddie," Baird said, greeting Alec as he joined him. "Didn't realize you could still run with those arthritic hips and knees."

"I have no arthritis, old boy, and if you remember, I could always outrun you. I'm sure I still can."

"Are you challenging me to a race?"

"I can't. I'd hate to show you up on Christmas."

"It's not Christmas until tomorrow. Let's see who is the faster man." And then Baird took off, at a full sprint, and then Alec came charging, dogs dashing ahead of them, and they ran hard, running until they were breathless and laughing and because Baird never took chances, and he didn't like to lose, Baird ran sideways into Alec, knocking him hard to his feet to ensure Alec couldn't win.

Alec howled in outrage. The dogs danced around barking. Baird dropped to the frosty ground next to Alec laughing hard. "Oh, that was fun. Should we do it again?"

Alec glowered at Baird. "Only if you want me to send you flying."

"I'd like to see you try."

Alec threw himself on top of Baird and they were wrestling on the crunchy grass as if boys again. They'd always been evenly matched in terms of strength and Alec, despite the stressful past few weeks, held his own against Baird, who outweighed him by a stone or more. Neither could completely defeat the other. They took turns getting the upper hand only to lose it again. Finally, they were both worn out, and they lay back on the ground staring up at the blue sky.

"You're a good friend," Baird said to Alec.

"No, you're the good friend," Alec returned. "Thank you for taking care of things here while I was in London."

"Anything, anytime," Baird answered sitting up and brushing the dried twigs and leaves from his shoulders and back.

"Did Ella like the surprise last night when you got home from Chesterfield?" Alec asked, sitting up, too.

"She did. Thank you so much for arranging that. We'd had a strange conversation at the restaurant and then we came home to the decorated cottage and it helped."

Alec eyed him as he got to his feet. "It was your idea."

Baird rose, too. "I couldn't have pulled it off without help. Who did all the work? I want to take care of them."

"Mrs. Booth's kids and, Darren, Mr. Trimble's assistant, did most of it. I drove Cara down so she could see." Alec shook his head. "You made her cry. She was so touched that you'd plan a surprise like that for Ella."

"But Ella isn't to know. This isn't about me. It's about making her Christmas here special."

"Understood. We're keeping your secret. Our lips are sealed."

Baird returned to the cottage to shower and found Ella sitting in the cottage next to the Christmas tree. She had made herself coffee and beamed at him when he entered.

"Isn't this just so lovely?" she said happily, reaching out to lightly touch one of the tree branches. "I don't even want to go up to the house now."

"Your sister would be disappointed."

"I know. But you have to admit this is adorable. A cottage Christmas. It's just perfect."

Baird smiled at her. "I have to shower, but let me know when you're ready to go to the house, and I'll go with you."

She nodded, and he paused to take one last look at her curled up in the chair gently touching the tree, her fingertip brushing the needles.

It felt good to have made her happy.

ELLA SAT ON the top step in the shadows of the upper landing, listening to Baird sing in the shower. She'd never heard him even hum before, and to hear him in the bathroom, singing the most achingly beautiful song, made her creep up the stairs to listen.

He had a gorgeous voice. Who knew? It was deep and textured, and he sang with emotion, so much emotion. It wasn't a song she'd heard before, and she didn't know if it was a hymn or a carol, but her eyes teared listening to him. She didn't want him to stop.

Last night had been intense, and then they'd returned to the beautifully decorated cottage, and she hadn't known what to think or feel. The decorations had been lovely, and it had been such a sweet surprise from Alec and Cara, but Baird signing this particular melody completely undid her.

How to be angry with him?

How to wish he was someone else?

How to wish he'd make different choices?

She didn't want to change him. She didn't want him to be anyone but himself, but it hurt knowing they weren't going to be more than what they were.

King of Kings, most Holy One, God the Son, Eternal One...

Her eyes teared and she held her breath, overwhelmed by the sacred beauty of the song, the season, and the reverence in Baird's voice.

He might say he was hard and bad. He might say he was selfish and a terrible partner, but she didn't believe it, she couldn't believe it. How could he be so hard and bad, so selfish and terrible when he sang like he belonged to a heavenly choir?

She heard the water turn off and Ella scrambled back down the stairs, not wanting to be caught outside the bathroom listening. She drew a blanket over her lap, her eyes still burning, her heart aching.

She loved him. She'd loved him from the moment she laid eyes on him. But it didn't mean they were meant to be together. It just meant she'd always be his friend, always his fan, always in his corner, even if that meant from Bellingham.

Chapter Eight

Up at the house, everyone had something to do to get ready for Christmas tomorrow, everyone but Uncle Frederick who was taking an extended nap in the library in front of the television. Earlier that morning, Ella and Baird took the Christmas presents Cara wanted to the house and then stayed for breakfast.

Ella, not being needed for a couple of hours, snuck out and walked into Bakewell to attend the eleven a.m. service at the nearest church. She didn't attend church often at home anymore, but it felt good to take a break and go this morning. She welcomed the calm, and the opportunity to be quiet, and pray, sing, and listen to the sermon.

You don't have to have all the answers, she reminded herself.

You don't have to know everything today.

Ella slipped away as soon as the service ended and walked back to Langley Park. Hanging up her coat in the mudroom and easing off her boots, she padded down the hall and peeked in to the kitchen where she saw Alec and Baird in flour covered aprons, apparently making something—baking something—from the bowls of freshly washed berries to the flour and sugar cannisters, along with an impressive number of measuring cups.

Alec spotted her in the doorway and shooed her away. "You will have to wait until later to see," he said. "It's a secret."

"And this secret is for tonight?" she asked.

"No spoilers," Baird answered. "Please continue on your way. This is men's work."

Apparently, men's work involved lots of spills, and a dozen different bowls and pans. "I'm just looking for Cara. Do either of you know where she happened to disappear to?" she asked.

"The wrapping room," Alec said, briefly glancing up. "It's the first door on the left, once you've taken a right to the family wing."

"So, the same floor as your bedroom, only this is the first door down that hallway, on the left-hand side."

Baird and Alex exchanged glances. "Isn't that what I said?" Alec asked Baird.

Baird shrugged. "I understood it."

Ella rolled her eyes and left, returning to the center hall where she quickly climbed the grand curving staircase to the second floor. Opening the first door on her left—once she'd turned left at the top of the stairs, not right—she found Cara seated at a long table with wrapping paper, ribbons and bows spread out in every direction.

"So, this is the wrapping room," Ella said, closing the door behind her because the hallway was much colder than the room, which had a little space heater in it to keep Cara warm.

"It's my personal sitting room," Cara answered, "but I rarely use it. I'm not sure what I'm supposed to do with a personal sitting room. In the past, the Countess Sherbourne might have gathered with friends or female family members. She might have worked on embroidery or practiced her watercolors. I do none of that, so the room is usually neglected, but it does make a wonderful space to write Christmas cards or wrap gifts."

"If this was my room, I'd fill that wall with books," Ella said, glancing around and seeing open space for bookshelves. "I'd put a chaise there by the window for reading, and maybe a desk for some writing. And I wouldn't let anyone come in. It would be my private domain."

"Poor Ella, the youngest of five, never had any privacy." Cara finished the bow on the package and set it aside. "There is already a library here. If you were the countess here, wouldn't you want to add your books to the library?"

Ella sat down in a chair not far from where Cara was working. "No, I'd want my books in a room that was mine, and then I'd decorate it the way I liked it. The house I share with my roommates came furnished, and most of my favorite books are in boxes in Mom and Dad's garage. Someday, I hope to pull them out and put them on display."

"Soon," Cara reminded her. "So, where have you been? Were you hiding down at the cottage with your own decorations?"

"No. I went to church in the village. It was really lovely. I feel better now."

Cara set down the scissors. "Are you upset about anything? Has Baird done—"

"No. This isn't about Baird. He's fine. Really. We're not fighting as much as we were." Ella glanced around the room, which was very formal with a gold framed mirror over the marble hearth, light blue toile wallpaper, a blue floral embroidered fire screen, and a half dozen gold framed portraits on the wall. "Does it ever seem strange that you live here now?"

"Every day." Cara looked up and smiled. "But I'd never tell Alec that. It would hurt his feelings. My happiness is so important to him."

"Maybe you just need a room you can fix up your way? Make it less formal, less impersonal. Like this room. It's frozen in time, trapped in the nineteenth century."

"I don't mind. I rarely come in here."

"But would you enjoy it more if it was your style?"

Cara shrugged. "I'd rather focus on the nursery. That's a huge space and it hasn't had anything done to it since before Alec was born."

"Where is the nursery?"

"It's up another floor, and then down the hall, around a

corner, near a set of servants stairs which are ridiculously steep." Cara reached for another box to wrap. "The old nursery was placed as far from the parents as possible so they wouldn't be inconvenienced."

"That's not going to work for you."

"No, definitely not. I do have plans to make things comfortable, too. I'd like to convert the countess's suite into a nursery. It's on this floor, in this wing. The bedroom is huge with lots of lovely natural light. I think it would be ideal for the children, especially when just babies."

"Does Alec have any objection?"

"I haven't spoken to him about it. I thought I'd wait until we got through the holidays and have our checkup with the doctor in mid-January. If everything is good then, I'll bring it up, and if he approves, we will get the renovations started."

"You think he'll approve?"

"Absolutely. He wants the children near us, especially during the night. He didn't have access to his parents as a young child and he's going to be a very different parent than his father. By the way, have you seen the guys?" Cara asked, reaching for yet another gift to wrap.

"Oh, yes. They are in the kitchen making a huge mess. I think it's something we're supposed to eat later."

Cara grinned. "Did it happen to have strawberries?"

"I did see quite a few berries, as well as berry juice, and smashed berries on the side of a bowl, and a strawberry on the floor."

"They're making Eton mess for us tonight. It's a first for both of them, so this should be fun."

"Mess as in mess?"

"Yes, and Eton as in school." Cara turned the wrapped gift over before reaching for a narrow dark green ribbon. "It's a popular summer dessert when fruit is plentiful, but it's quite festive for Christmas. I'm rather fond of it, but then, I've only ever had Mrs. Johnson's, and everything she makes is delicious."

"I'm looking forward to their mess," Ella answered, rising. "And even if it's dreadful, I will say nice things. As a good sister-in-law should."

ELLA HELPED MRS. Booth set the table for Christmas Eve dinner, aware that Mrs. Booth was joining her children that evening for a special pre-holiday dinner at a restaurant in Bakewell that was highly regarded. Mrs. Booth would then have the next four days off, and Mrs. Johnson had been invited to join the Trimbles for dinner tomorrow at their house, and they'd pushed their dinner time back so that Mrs. Johnson could plate the Sherbournes Christmas dinner first.

Ella had not yet eaten in the formal dining room and was awed by the soaring ceiling and the enormous fireplaces at either end of the lofty room. Mrs. Booth had already spread a long red cloth on the table and was now adding the silverware.

"Cara told us that you have a big dinner in the United States for Christmas Eve and Christmas Day," Mrs. Booth said, quickly buffing each of the flatware before she set it down. "That must be a lot of cooking for your mother to do."

"It is," Ella agreed, adding the crystal goblets to the table, happy to have something useful to do. "Fortunately, my mother has three sisters and two of them live close, so we always spend holidays with family, and Mom has her sisters in the kitchen helping cook. But now that Mom and my aunts are getting older, they're wanting to simplify, especially as my brothers' wives aren't wanting to take on the responsibility of feeding everyone."

"How many gather at your house for Christmas dinner?"

Ella counted in her head, remembering how last year Cara wasn't there. "It varies, but usually between nineteen and twenty-four, which would be easy to seat here, but we usually have to put up additional tables in the living room and then a children's table in the family room."

"And what do you eat for Christmas?"

"My father prefers prime rib, but my mother likes turkey, so we alternate every year."

"The Sherbournes have turkey on Christmas Day and then prime rib and Yorkshire puddings for New Year's."

"Do you know what we're having tonight?"

"Duck and roasted vegetables. Potatoes—Lord Sherbourne likes his potatoes—and then the special dessert."

"The mess."

Mrs. Booth laughed out loud. "The Eton mess, yes, and I saw the kitchen. So did Mrs. Johnson, but she's happy to have Lord Sherbourne home and didn't mind the fuss…or the mess." She winked at Ella before glancing back at the table, counting the place settings. "I think we are short a place setting. Do you mind bringing in another plate and stemware from the closet downstairs? I confess, my legs are tired today."

"I don't mind at all. You should have put me to work sooner!"

THE TOWERING CHRISTMAS tree in the green drawing room was lit, and dozens of pretty packages nestled at the base. Candles flickered on the mantle, and Emma was at the piano in the music room playing lovely traditional carols.

Uncle Frederick, Aunt Dorothy, Cara, and Alex had gathered in the Music Room to enjoy the impromptu concert while Mrs. Johnson put the finishing touches to her Christmas Eve dinner. Ella was still enjoying being useful and was assisting Mrs. Johnson with putting last-minute things on table now that Mrs. Booth had gone to dinner.

After placing the bottles of opened red wine on the table,

Ella adjusted the fragrant Christmas centerpiece she'd helped Mrs. Booth create earlier made from fresh pine branches, pine cones, and small oranges studded with whole cloves. Three tall dark red candles rose from the middle of the centerpiece, their soft light created a beautiful glow, captured by the elegant stemware and fine China.

The sound of the doorbell caught her by surprise. Was someone expected? Or maybe it was a late delivery, perhaps with some of the gifts Cara had ordered. With Mrs. Johnson in the kitchen and Mrs. Booth gone, Ella went to the door and opened it. A middle-aged man stood on the threshold in a winter coat, a driving cap in his hands.

"Is Alec available?" he asked, his English accent different from Baird's, and even different from Alec's.

"Yes," she said. "May I tell him whose here?"

He hesitated briefly. "James Phelps."

Her stomach knotted and her heart fell. She recognized the name. Footsteps sounded in the entry hall. Baird had come to see who was at the door.

"A James Phelps is here," Ella said to Baird.

She wanted to ask Baird if it was the same man who took money from Alec's firm, but she didn't have to. Baird's hard expression revealed his displeasure.

"Would you like to come in?" Ella asked, turning back to Mr. Phelps. "Perhaps you'd like to sit while I get Alec."

"He's fine where he is," Baird said quietly. "I'll go get Alec."

Ella closed the door behind Mr. Phelps. She didn't know what to say to him, and she didn't think he would speak to her and then he suddenly asked, "Are you Lady Sherbourne's sister?"

Ella nodded.

"You've come from America," he added.

Ella nodded again. "Just for the holidays."

"I heard she hasn't been well."

Ella lifted her head and gave the man an incredulous look. "Then why on earth—" But she broke off and pressed her lips together.

For a long minute, she just stood in the entry looking at Mr. Phelps while he stared at the floor.

Finally, Baird was returning with Alec, and Ella slipped away.

BAIRD REMAINED. THERE was no way he was going to leave Alec with the dregs of society. He was so angry he wanted to grab James and pin him to the floor and then throttle him until he cried like a baby.

"Good evening, James," Alec said coolly. "This is a surprise."

"I imagine it is."

"Would you like to sit down? The drawing room is far warmer than here in the hall."

"I'm not staying long," James answered, turning his hat once, and then again. "I've just come to apologize. I had to do it in person. I had to apologize so you could hear how sorry I am." He lifted his head and he looked into Alec's eyes. "I'd like to say I don't know why I took the money, but I do."

Silence followed, and Baird could tell Phelps was nervous, but was certain it was all an act. He certainly felt no sympathy for the man.

James took a breath. "I made some bad decisions financially, and I was in a tough position, short of funds, and I thought I'll just borrow a little bit and pay it back as soon as I can. It didn't work out that way, though. I couldn't pay it back, and I was still in the hole, and so I borrowed more, and then some more, and by the time I realized just how much I'd taken, I knew I'd ruined myself, and maybe you. Every day, I wanted to tell you. Every day, I vowed I'd come to you and confess what I'd done. But when I saw you in the office, you reminded me so much of your father, and he was so very good to me. He believed in me when no one else did. And instead of admitting to the truth, I just pretended it wasn't me. Why did it have to be me?"

"Because it was you," Baird said harshly, unable to keep his silence.

He'd known James Phelps a very long time. Phelps had been a frequent visitor here when the old earl was alive. And the earl had given Phelps tremendous support and encouragement, encouragement he didn't show to Alec. Alec was constantly having to prove himself, and even if Alec shrugged it off, it bothered Baird.

"I know," James said. "I'm not trying to justify my behavior, either. What I've done is terrible, truly terrible. I don't have the means to pay it all back. Most of it is gone to cover those gambling debts, and the rest is in the bank, being saved for Helen to help take care of her and the children when I'm no longer around."

"Does Helen know?" Alec asked.

James shook his head. "I'm heading home tonight to tell her. She thinks I've been on a business trip."

"I talked to her, you know. She said she didn't know where you were."

"I know." Ruddy color washed through James's face. "I said I was job interviewing and didn't want you to know."

"So many lies," Baird said. "You had to know they would catch up with you?"

For a moment, James didn't speak and then when he did, his voice cracked. "I don't feel bad for me, but I feel terrible for Helen and the kids. They don't deserve this. It will be hard for them when the truth comes out."

Baird shook his head. "You should have thought of that before."

Alec gestured to the green drawing room. "Let's go sit by the fire. You're cold, James. There's no reason to have you standing here shivering."

Alec and James took seats in the armchairs and Baird stood at the fireplace, needing to keep his distance. He was so angry on Alec's behalf. James had put Alec through hell the past week. And to just show up here on Christmas Eve and act as if an apology could make everything right?

"So, you're gambling again, James," Alec said quietly.

James lifted his head, looked at Alec and then down again. "You know about your dad helping me out before?"

"My father never told me, but I saw it in the personal ledger my father kept for his personal accounts. He took care of your debts five or six years ago."

"Seven," James said. "And I promised him I'd never gamble again. And I didn't go near the horses, didn't place bets, not until last spring when I had a really good feeling about a horse, and I thought one bet won't hurt, and I was so sure the horse would win."

"The horse didn't?"

James made a rough sound. "No, he did. And it's such a high when you win, it feels so good, and I thought whatever I win will be for Helen. I'd take her on a proper vacation, and maybe get Jimmy a car for uni. And I won once more, but then I began to lose. I should have stopped then. Instead, you think your luck will change, and it only takes one good win and you'll be on top again."

Alec rose and walked to the sideboard with the tray of bottles and glasses. He poured a splash of sherry into three glasses and carried one to Baird and then handed another to

James and kept the third for himself. "I wish you would have just told me," he said. "I would have helped you."

"I know. I was too ashamed."

Silence stretched and the only sound was the fire crackling. "What will you tell Helen when you get home?" Alec asked.

"The truth." James shrugged. "I need to tell them, and then I'll turn myself in. I don't want to hide anymore. I don't want to live like this anymore. I know I owe you a great deal of money, but I will do my best to pay you back, even if it takes me the rest of my life."

Alec studied the man who had been at his side every day for the past twelve years. "You need therapy not prison."

"I embezzled funds. Not just from you, but others. It's a crime and I must be held accountable."

"My father loved you like a son."

James looked away, a sheen in his eyes. "I'm glad he's not alive to witness this."

"So, the money isn't all gone?"

"More than half of it is."

"You need to pay back the clients first, and then my aunts and uncle. I won't ask you to pay me back. I doubt that you can, and I don't want you to spend the rest of your life struggling with that burden. Instead, I want you to get help, proper help. You can decide how much or how little you tell Helen about the missing funds. But she must know you need professional help, or your demons will eat you alive, and that's not fair for her, or your children."

"I didn't come here to be exonerated, Alec. You should press charges, Alec. Make a lesson out of me so others don't think—"

"That's not who I am. And I can't forget how much you meant to my father. I will not inflict on you or your family more pain. I want to keep this between us, and not let any of this become public. There's no reason to put your family through that kind of media circus. I like Helen and your kids, and I don't want them to suffer or be ashamed. I don't want them ashamed of you either."

James put his sherry down, untouched. "I have to tell them."

"Then that's up to you. But think about your family, James, put them first, not last."

A light step sounded in the hall and Cara was there, on the threshold between the music room and green room. "Happy Christmas, James," she said, entering the drawing room and approaching the men.

She stood next to Alec, her hands clasped in front of her. "Mrs. Johnson has been keeping dinner warm, but she can't keep warming it all night." Cara looked at James and smiled. "Stay for dinner, James. And before you say no, my sister has already added a place for you at the table. It's Christmas. You shouldn't be alone."

James rose and dipped his head. "Thank you for the invitation, but I will be heading home tonight. I'll have something to eat when I get there."

"I'm sure that won't be for hours," Cara protested. "At least have a little bite with us. You'll feel better driving."

Alec's dark head inclined. "Cara is right. Join us, in the true spirit of Chritmas. You don't have to stay for all the courses. Have some soup, salad, and take off when you're ready."

Chapter Nine

Baird didn't think he'd had a less enjoyable Christmas Eve in years. He was angry, so angry he knew he didn't belong here.

James Phelps should not have been invited to stay for dinner. James Phelps didn't deserve such compassion. Baird couldn't imagine how Alec forgave him and brought him into his home on Christmas Eve.

The world was filled with problems, problems humans created and inflicted on each other—and the planet, from the earth to the animals, to the seas filled with poisons and plastic. Humans needed to take responsibility and do better, and while Baird was glad James had come to Langley Park to confess what he'd done, that didn't mean the crime hadn't been committed, and James should still be held accountable.

Baird wasn't good at forgiving, and he was even worse at forgetting.

He had faith, but it wasn't the kind that rewarded those who stole, who hurt, who committed crimes. A criminal needed to be punished, and in this case, serve time. Just apologizing wasn't good enough. An apology didn't make everything right.

Sitting at the table with Alec's family and interloper James, Baird felt rage. He couldn't even look in James's direction. He could barely look around the table, too afraid the others would see just how upset he was.

It was a relief when James rose and said he had to be on the road, that his family was home expecting him.

Alec walked James out, and Ella cleared the dinner dishes from the table. Baird brought in the platters and serving bowls.

"You're upset," Ella said to him as he placed the bowls and platter on the counter.

"Seething might be a more accurate word," he said tightly, running his hand over his face and jaw. "I wanted to reach across the table and throttle him all dinner. I wanted to make him suffer."

Ella began scraping a plate into the trash bin. "But you didn't."

"Out of respect for Cara."

"Which was very considerate of you." Ella scraped another, placing them in a stack in the sink.

"I can't believe Alec is just going to let Phelps off the hook. It's wrong. I believe in showing compassion for those in need, but Phelps was the senior vice president of Langley Investments, his salary in the hundreds of thousands of pounds each year. He has great benefits, a loving family, and more to the point, has been saved from ruin once before by

Alec's father. And despite all of that, he still embezzled money from his Langley clients? *And* the Sherbourne family? Unforgiveable."

Ella rinsed her hands and turned to Baird. "You're surprised that Alec handled it this way?"

"Stunned." Baird shook his head. "Alec wouldn't have been this soft a year ago. He would have taken legal measures against Phelps, he would have exposed him, he would have pressed charges. But marrying Cara has changed Alec. Love has made him soft—"

Ella's eyes widened. "How dare you! What an awful thing to say about anyone, much less your best friend." She looked at Baird, appalled. "In case you've forgotten, it's Alec's firm. He is entitled to make the decisions he thinks best, and I don't think his decisions are because he's *married* and has become soft or weak. You should be ashamed of yourself," she said tightly, walking past him to return to the dining room.

Baird growled in frustration in the empty kitchen. He put some of the leftovers into containers for the refrigerator, not yet wanting to join everyone in the dining room. He was still tidying the kitchen when Alec entered the kitchen.

"It's been an interesting evening," Alec said.

Baird could see the fatigue in Alec's expression. Tonight clearly hadn't been easy for him, either.

"You can't just let him walk free," Baird said quietly.

"It's what my father would have wanted."

"Alec, if you hadn't caught on last week, he would have kept stealing. He didn't stop because he felt guilty. He only stopped because you found out, and instead of coming clean then, he went into hiding."

"If I press charges, it all becomes public knowledge. I'm trying to protect my clients and the company."

"And who protects you, Alec?"

Alec smiled wearily at his childhood friend. "You do, Baird." He drew a deep breath and straightened, squaring his shoulders. "Is it time for pudding?"

Baird and Alec retrieved the tray of bowls from the big refrigerator and carried the bowls of Eton mess to the dining table.

Everyone exclaimed over the scarlet berries, whipping cream, and meringue confection, and with the tiny mint leaf and sugared cranberry on top of each—the garnishes courtesy Mrs. Johnson—it was a most festive and delicious Christmas pudding.

After dinner, the first part of the evening was spent in the green drawing room playing cards, and then when Cara couldn't stop yawning, Alec took her upstairs and stayed with her there. Ella, Frederick, and the aunts decided to watch a Christmas movie in the library. Uncle Frederick fell asleep right away, snoring softly in his armchair, only waking when the movie ended. Ella was aware that Baird had disappeared when Alec and Cara left, but she'd expected him to return for the movie. He never did.

Now at ten, the candles were being blown out and the house lights turned off. The aunts were upstairs. Frederick was in his bed. Ella went to the mudroom to get her jacket and discovered Baird was already there, getting the dogs ready for one last walk.

Baird looked at her and she looked at him, not knowing what to say. She was still upset at him, still in disbelief that he'd say such a thing—not just to her, but to anyone.

"Will an apology help?" Baird asked her stiffly, not looking or sounding the least remorseful.

"Do you dislike Cara so much?" Ella asked grimly.

"This isn't about Cara. It's about relationships and marriage. If you don't yet know, I'm quite cynical about relationships and do my best to avoid attending weddings—I find them farcical."

"Oh, come on!"

"Forty percent of marriages in the UK end in divorce. Even higher for second marriages."

"But you were Alec's best man."

Baird made a rough sound. "Because he's my best friend. I might be a cynical bastard, but he's like a brother to me, and I'll always be there for him, in good times and bad."

"Marriage being bad for him."

Baird opened the mudroom door. "Are you coming?"

She yanked her coat on. "Only because I need to end up at the cottage."

His lips compressed. "And I wondered if your temper

matched your red hair."

"And now you know," she flashed.

The dogs bounded out into the night and Ella shut the door behind her. "What is it like going through life so cynical?"

"Good. I generally win. In and out of the courtroom."

"Lucky you."

"But it's why my clients come to me. It's why I'm in demand. I fight for my clients, and I fight for my friends."

"Does that include Cara?"

"Of course. But in the beginning, I was skeptical about how quickly Alec fell in love with her. Everything happened very quickly between them. They'd known each other only a few weeks before Alec proposed."

"And Cara was an American, and not from a similar background."

Baird shrugged. "I did wonder if she was a gold digger."

Ella didn't like that description at all. "When did you realize she wasn't?"

"As soon as I met her. But even if I had disapproved it wouldn't have mattered. Alec was smitten. He wasn't going to lose her. All I had to do was draw up the prenuptial agreement—"

"He made her sign a prenup?" Ella interrupted horrified.

"Cara didn't mind. She understood that Langley Park and the various Sherbourne estates had to remain in the family—"

"And you put together the prenup? This was your doing?"

"If it wasn't me, it would have been another attorney. He had to do it. It's to protect the family."

"Cara was becoming his family!"

He shook his head, exasperated. "I should have never mentioned it. I thought you were reasonable, and you'd understand the legal ramifications for both of them, and how they both needed to be protected, which is what a prenuptial agreement does."

"And yet you've already said you are Alec's friend and you're loyal to him."

"I brought in an attorney to meet with Cara and explain everything to her. There was no intimidation, no coercion. You are the one making it sound sordid."

"Because it is sordid! A prenup assumes that the marriage won't work. It might as well be a curse."

"That is dramatic and inaccurate. A prenup protects everyone, including future children. No one wants a family torn apart, much less dragged through court."

"I suppose a lawyer would look at it that way." She shook her head, so aggravated she couldn't think straight. "I can't do this, not tonight, not on Christmas Eve. I'm going to go to bed and hopefully in the morning this was all just a bad dream."

"I'm not the villain, Ella."

"Maybe not, but you're certainly not the hero, Baird."

BAIRD WAS STILL awake in his cottage bedroom when he received a late-night call from his dad in Melbourne saying Aunt Kate, his dad's sister, was having a hard time and was there any way Baird could pop in and see her? Maybe spend Christmas Day with her?

The last thing Baird wanted to do at eleven was begin a five hour drive, but he had a soft spot for his Aunt Kate, a recent widow, whose only child moved to America fifteen years ago.

"I'll be there tomorrow," Baird told his father. "Don't say anything to her," he added. "I'll surprise her in the morning."

After hanging up, Baird quickly dressed and packed his travel bag. He glanced around his now empty room, making sure he had everything before descending the stairs and heading outside to start the drive home.

He hadn't planned on leaving in the night, but once he was on the freeway, which was virtually empty at midnight, he rolled his window down and drove fast, letting the cold air clear his head.

This was the right thing to do, go home. Extract himself from Langley Park. And Ella. He didn't want to battle her, and he didn't agree with her, and no matter how mad she got at him, it wasn't going to change him, or his point of view.

ELLA WOKE UP and stretched, sleepy but rested. Had she finally kicked jet lag?

Lying in her warm bed, she listened, aware of the stillness. It was Christmas. Christmas morning. She listened again, wondering if maybe she could hear Baird singing, wanting to hear his lovely voice again, singing another haunting hymn, but the cottage was quiet, and then she remembered how she'd gone to bed mad at Baird and guilt filled her. She'd been a little harsh, but he'd been impossible. Who could hate marriage that much?

Did he owe her an apology, or did she owe him one? It was confusing but also disappointing. She didn't like fighting with him and last night they'd quarreled twice. With someone else she wouldn't have even bothered. She would have bit her tongue and continued on, but Baird wasn't just anyone and she couldn't believe he'd be so negative... so pessimistic.

How to reconcile someone who sang like an angel with a man who couldn't yield or bend?

She closed her eyes, refusing to even think about the prenup. That still made her see red, but it was Christmas, and a new day. Forgiveness was important, and so was compassion. Maybe she could forgive Baird for being difficult and unreasonable. She smiled faintly, knowing he thought it was the other way around, that she was emotional and unreasonable. She was the problem.

They were a pair, weren't they? Ella smiled a little bigger. She'd apologize when she saw him. She'd do her best to keep her million opinions to herself.

Ella bundled up in a big sweater and peeked downstairs. It was cold, and everything was dark. The little tree hadn't been plugged in. There were no candles lit and the fire in the hearth had burned out. The kitchen was equally dark, and no coffee brewing.

Ella glanced to the front door. Baird's coat was not hanging there. The coffee cup he'd used the past several days wasn't on the counter or in the sink. There were no papers or books anywhere. Downstairs was spotless.

Worried, she went back upstairs, walking down the hall to Baird's room and lightly rapped on the door. There was no answer. She opened the door and peeked in. His bed had not been slept in. Or if he'd slept in it, he'd made it up and removed all of his things. There was no sign of him anymore. No clothes, no suitcase, nothing on the nightstand, nothing anywhere. He was gone.

Ella went to his window and looked out, her gaze going to the house and the gravel driveway curious if she could see Baird's car, but a tree blocked part of the driveway, and then the old stablemasters house which had become an office for the Christmas tours, with the second floor becoming Mrs. Johnson's home.

He wasn't here anymore.

Ella didn't know how she knew, but she knew. He'd left, just as he'd left last August, the morning after the wedding. Instead of attending the brunch, instead of saying goodbye, he woke up early and returned to the Seattle airport. And now he was gone again. One more abrupt departure that no one saw coming, least of all her.

Ella took a quick breath, her chest tight, pins and needles in her middle. It hurt, the way he just left, but this was who he was, and she'd seen his true colors—twice. She should be relieved he'd left.

She was relieved, she silently insisted. And she wasn't going to cry.

CHRISTMAS MORNING AT the house was nice—mature and a little dull but civilized. No small children tearing packages open. No stockings overflowing. No crumbs and half eaten cinnamon rolls left on holiday plates.

Cara smiled at Ella from across the drawing room, and Ella smiled back. It was her fake brave smile, the big bright one when she didn't want anyone to know how she felt on the inside. It was a smile she used sometimes when teaching. It was a smile she wore when listening to her advisor destroy her dissertation telling her it wasn't strong enough, she wasn't digging deep enough.

She had that smile on her face today because she wasn't

miserable. She wasn't tortured. She wasn't in a bad place. But she did feel a little sad, and a little regretful.

"We are down to our last gift," Alec said, picking up a white box with gold stars and checking the nametag. "Ella, it's for you."

Ella rose and took the gift from Alec and sat down again. She didn't recognize the handwriting. It wasn't Alec's handwriting, and it wasn't Cara's. It wasn't the aunts or uncle, either as she had already opened small gifts from them.

Tearing the wrapping paper away from the box, she saw it was a pale silver clothing box. She carefully lifted the lid off and pulled the tissue paper back revealing a folded pink cardigan, the edges finished in a darker pink crochet trim. It was a very delicate little trim. It also happened to be the sweater she had seen two days ago in Bakewell when shopping with Baird for a sweater for Dorothy.

Lifting the cardigan from the box she gave it a little shake, admiring how the fabric buttons were the same pink as the jacket.

"What a pretty sweater," Cara said from her seat on the couch. "Who's it from?"

"Baird," Ella said softly, carefully folding the sweater and placing it back in the box.

A knot filled her throat, and she smoothed the sweater, stunned. She hadn't expected anything from him, never mind the lovely hand-knit sweater she'd admired in a

Bakewell shop he hadn't even gone into with her. How had he known? How had he managed it?

Cara looked at Alec. "What did Baird give you, honey?"

"Nothing," Alec answered. "What did he give you, darling?"

Ella flushed, knowing exactly what they were doing. "I don't know why he gave the sweater to me. I didn't give him anything."

"What a beautiful cardigan, and in your favorite color," Dorothy said.

"Oh, you should put it on," Emma said.

But Ella looked at Dorothy. "How do you know I love pink?"

Dorothy smiled kindly at her. "It's what you wear whenever you're happy."

CHRISTMAS DINNER WAS served midafternoon right after the Royal Christmas Message, which they all watched on the library television. Uncle Frederick looked a little emotional at the end, acknowledging that he missed the Queen. Her Royal Majesty had served them well for so many years, and he was forever grateful to her.

Mrs. Johnson had watched the message on the kitchen TV and, as soon as it was over, began to serve dinner as she knew everyone was moving to the dining room. The turkey was perfect, as were the roast potatoes and cranberries, the winter squash and other sides. Everyone was in good spirits and there was a great deal of discussion about how well the King looked, and what a good speech he gave, yet how could they forget the late Queen? At the end of the meal, Mrs. Johnson appeared with the Christmas pudding doused in brandy, and carried the burning cake into the dining room to lots of admiration.

Aunt Emma insisted on slicing the cake, and then Dorothy poured a generous serving of brandy cream over each slice before it was passed around.

It was Ella's first Christmas pudding and it was good, but very rich. She was glad that Mrs. Johnson's recipe—which was an upgraded version of the old Sherbourne family recipe—had no nuts, and not an excessive amount of candied peel which neither Cara nor Ella was fond of. But otherwise, the pudding was traditional and decadent, with spices and dried fruit and that lovely brandy cream, which made Ella think of Dickens and Victorian Christmas traditions, originating from Queen Victoria's marriage to her beloved German husband, Albert.

The family scattered after the dinner, some to nap, some to watch television, and in Alec's case, to read by the fire in the green drawing room. He liked the drawing room in the afternoon, the winter sun creating ideal reading conditions, but he could also keep an eye on Cara who was half reclining on the couch, talking to Ella.

"You've been so quiet today," Cara said. "Is this about Baird leaving?"

Ella's chest ached. She didn't want to think about him, and yet he'd been on her mind all day. "I hate that he leaves and doesn't say goodbye."

"He sent a text, explaining that his aunt needed him."

"You believe him?"

"Yes." Cara frowned. "Why wouldn't you believe him?"

Ella glanced away, looking at the Christmas tree and then the wreath hanging on red ribbon in each of the tall drawing room windows. "We had some words."

Cara pushed up into a sitting position. "Why?"

"He said the most outrageous things, ridiculous things, and he made me mad."

"That's not necessarily hard to do. You are a bit of a hot head."

"Not really."

Cara gave her a look, and Ella sighed and scooted lower in her chair, her voice dropping as she definitely didn't want Alec to overhear. "He thinks marriage made Alec soft," Ella said, nearly spitting the words out. "And he's supposed to be Alec's best friend."

Cara didn't seem bothered. "They've known each other since they were boys. He's entitled to think what he wants … that is the best friend's prerogative, wouldn't you agree?"

"He hates marriage."

"I don't think he hates marriage. He's just seen too much

to believe marriage is the answer to everything."

Ella was just getting more upset. "He's so cynical."

"He is," Cara agreed. She hesitated a moment, picking her words with care. "Why does that bother you so much?"

Ella sat forward, closing the distance between her and Cara. "Did he really make you sign a prenup?"

Cara blinked, surprised. "Is that why you're so upset?"

"One of the reasons." Ella felt terribly close to tears. "So, he did. He made you."

"No, Ella, no." Cara put her hand on Ella's knee. "No one made me do anything. I chose to sign the agreement to protect Alec and the Sherbourne legacy. If our marriage ended, I would never want to take any of his family property. Alec didn't buy Langley Park. It's been in the family for hundreds of years. It must stay in the family."

"So, if your marriage ended, Alec keeps everything, and you walk away with nothing?"

Ella's voice must have risen because suddenly Alec's head lifted and he glanced over at them, brow creasing.

Cara lowered her voice. "This isn't the best time or place to discuss this, Ella, but I have been well provided for. I would not be a poor woman. I wouldn't be on the streets. And in light of the fact that I am pregnant, the children would always be shared by us. I did agree to raise them here, and then once they reach the age to attend university, they could choose for themselves if they wanted to go to college here, or study in the States." Cara's gaze searched Ella's. "I'm disappointed in Baird for sharing with you that we signed a prenuptial, but I'm even more disappointed that you have made this a point of contention between the two of you. It's really no one's business but Alec's and mine."

CHRISTMAS DAY HAD come to a close and Ella was about to return to the cottage with her little pile of Christmas gifts when Alec said he was going to walk the dogs. Did Ella want to join him?

She hesitated and then said yes, provided they could pass the cottage so she could leave her gifts there and collect her cap and gloves.

The dogs were elated to be out walking with Alec, dashing ahead and then returning. Lady didn't dash much, but she kept close to Alec's side, looking up at him with adoring eyes.

At the cottage, Alec waited outside while Ella went in, turning on a few lights since it was already dark, leaving the gifts on the dining table and going up to her room for warmer things. Coming back down the stairs, she glanced around the dimly lit living area and the dark kitchen. The hearth had been cold all day. She missed the fire Baird had kept going, the warmth and light, the comforting crackling sound. She missed seeing Baird's coat on the hook by the door.

She missed Baird in a chair by the fire, his long legs stretched in front of him as he poured over documents from work.

She missed him, and it was that simple and that complicated. Was it her fault he'd gone? Had she been too harsh?

Her chest felt painfully tender as she snapped her coat up and tugged on her mittens. She missed Baird and this missing was different than the missing last August. This missing wasn't about heat or passion. It wasn't from a hot kiss but the abrupt loss of his company. They'd grown closer during the last five days and their day spent Christmas shopping and visiting the castle in Chesterfield had been special. Dinner had almost felt like a date. She had real feelings for him. So problematic, she admitted, stepping outside and closing the cottage door behind her.

She didn't even realize she'd sighed until Alec asked her if she was okay.

Ella looked up at him and managed a faint smile. "Yes. Why?"

"You've been on the quiet side all day," he said as they started walking in the direction of the village.

"Maybe today just seems anticlimactic after dinner last night." She glanced at him. "If I was shocked by the appearance of Mr. Phelps, I can't imagine how you felt."

Alec didn't immediately respond. They walked through a cluster of ancient trees, branches bare, and yet beautifully sculptural in the moonlight.

"So, you know who he is, and what's happened," Alec said eventually.

"Baird told me, and then when your relatives arrived, there was more discussion. Cara didn't know what had happened, not until you came home, though. Baird made sure of that."

"He's a good friend," Alec said simply.

They walked in silence, passing cottages glowing with light, all with cars parked out front. Some even had some Christmas decorations. But every one of the cottages on this side of the manor had been booked for the holidays.

"Do you want to ask me anything about the prenuptial agreement?" Alec said, as they neared the edge of his property. If they crossed the street, they'd be just a few minutes' walk from downtown Bakewell.

Ella flushed, uncomfortable and embarrassed. "Not really."

"I don't mind if you do. It's probably a shock for you. I've been raised knowing that any marriage of mine must have an agreement. For the last seventy-five years, every Sherbourne marriage has required the agreement, protecting the house and land, as well as other legacy properties. If the marriage fails, both parties will receive assets—the nonfamily member receives a sizable cash settlement, and the Sherbourne with the estates." He looked at Ella. "My children will have the same agreements when they marry. But I can assure you, Ella, that I love your sister with all my heart, and

I can't imagine my future without her. You do not have to worry for her."

Ella's eyes had filled with tears as he spoke, his voice so low and earnest, and it moved her, making her feel so many things at so many different levels. Cara was lucky to have him. Ella wished she hadn't been quite so harsh with Baird. She wished she and Baird were better at communicating.

She reached up, brushing away tears with the tips of her gloves. "Baird said one other thing." Her voice cracked. "He said marriage had made you soft." She wiped away another tear. "I was so mad at him for saying that. You aren't weak. You are strong, you are kind, and you are the best husband in the world."

Alec suddenly brought Ella in for a swift hug. "You shouldn't let my beastly friend get under your skin. He's tough, but he's very loyal, not just to me, but to Cara, too." He released Ella but kept a hand on her arm. "I can't imagine any friend more protective."

"He hates marriage."

Alec smiled, amused. "That's because he's never been in love." Alec whistled for Milo and Albert who'd nearly run beyond the estate gates. They immediately returned, racing at full speed.

"What about Fiona?" Ella said.

"He loved Fiona, but he wasn't in love with her. They were a very compatible couple, but there was no passion, no excitement, no friction, no emotional or intellectual challenge. It was easy between them, and they were happy until Fiona asked for more and Baird refused."

"Fiona must have been heartbroken."

"I think she was fine with it. The relationship had run its course and served its purpose."

"And what purpose was that?"

"Companionship without risk. It was easy. There was no need to grow or change." His lips curved, crookedly. "Love—real love—requires growth and change. It also means you fight for that person. You fight for the relationship. You don't just open the door and wave goodbye."

"Baird will never fight for love. It's not *logical*."

Alec laughed. "The first thing to know about Baird is that he isn't always logical. He just likes to think he is."

She kicked at a branch on the road and then kicked it again. "I hate that I fell for him at your wedding. I don't even know why I fell for him. He's really annoying. So frustrating."

Alec checked his smile. "That bad, hmm?"

Ella suddenly realized she was spilling her heart to Baird's best friend. "You won't tell him this, will you? It would only horrify him."

"No, it wouldn't. I suspect he feels the same."

"No offense, Alec. You're a wonderful brother-in-law, but in this case, I think you're wrong. Baird thinks it's just … chemistry … and it's all he's going to let it be. But that's not enough for me. I either want his whole heart, or I want nothing."

IF ALEC HAD thought his conversation with Ella would help, he was wrong. Ella went to bed Christmas night nauseous, her stomach heavy and knotted. She felt heartsick. Just awful. While she didn't exactly cry, her eyes burned dry and gritty. A painful lump filled her throat making it hard to swallow.

She regretted talking to Alec. She regretted talking to Cara. She regretted coming to England. She regretted falling for Baird.

She punched her pillow and then turned it over and punched it again.

What else could she regret?

Oh, that was easy.

Earning a PhD when she could have earned a masters. Staying in Bellingham for college instead of going away and learning to be more independent sooner.

And falling in love with the most gorgeous man she'd ever seen.

Tears seeped from beneath her lashes, and she pressed her face into the pillow to cover the sound of her crying. *Stop thinking, Ella. Sleep. Please.*

Chapter Ten

Baird took his Aunt Kate out for Christmas dinner. Reservations were impossible at such a late date. But remembering his chef client with a high-profile restaurant in Portobello, Baird texted him and apologetically asked if there was any way to get two in for Christmas dinner. His client, ever grateful that Baird actually saved his marriage, said yes, if they could be there at two.

Aunt Kate was thrilled to be taken to such a lovely restaurant in the very elegant seaside neighborhood. Portobello, established in the 1700s, was once a town in its own right but was now officially a suburb of Edinburgh, three miles east of the city center. Portobello faced the Firth of Forth, marked by a lovely long sandy beach and beautiful old architecture. In the early 1800s, Portobello became a popular holiday destination with bathing machines, and then later at the turn of the century, a bath house, but now was one of Edinburgh's posher neighborhoods.

As he and Aunt Kate walked along the promenade, the icy wind gusting, she periodically patted his arm, telling him how happy he had made her.

"When are you going to get married?" she asked as they turned around and began to retrace their steps to his car. "You are too lovely of a lad to remain single forever. You're almost thirty-five. It's time, isn't it?"

"Marriage isn't for everyone, Aunt Kate," he said, smiling down at her. "If I was married, I might not have been free to spend Christmas with you. Perhaps keeping your only nephew single would be a benefit to you."

She wagged a gloved finger at him. "That is not an acceptable excuse. I am sure any lass you married would be happy to drop in with you on Christmas, too."

Baird suddenly pictured Ella and thought Ella wouldn't mind. But then, Fiona wouldn't have minded, either. Only he'd never been inclined to take Fiona home or create holiday traditions with her. He'd never really thought about it until now.

How had he and Fiona celebrated Christmas? Who had they spent the day with?

Did they go to her family, or did they usually just spend it together? Frowning he tried to remember and then he realized why there were so few memories. She often worked Christmas. She tended to volunteer to take Christmas shifts so those with children could be home.

Fiona was a good woman, a loving woman, and a very skillful, knowledgeable surgeon. He couldn't find fault in her. He'd never felt as if their relationship was missing anything. And when she finally expressed she wanted more, he'd loved her enough to realize that if she wanted to marry and have children, then he needed to let her go. She deserved to be happy.

After driving his aunt back to her home, Baird walked her to the door and made sure she was safely inside, promising her he'd return and join her for lunch tomorrow, before driving back to his place.

Once in his own home, in his most comfortable lounging around pants, cozy sweater, and thick wool socks, Baird found it hard to unwind, thoughts of Fiona surprisingly intrusive.

He loved Fiona, he did.

But in all fairness, he'd never surprised her with a Christmas tree, or bought a frivolous gift simply to make her happy.

He'd never stayed awake at night replaying conversations in his head, angry and resentful. Her words had never hurt him. Her words had never moved him, either. They'd been calm and steady. Settled and focused. They'd been too busy for romance.

Whereas Ella…

Ella made him want to try, even if it wasn't comfortable or natural. Ella made him want to surprise her if only to see her eyes widen and that smile of hers that always did something to his chest, making it tight, and ache with emotions he barely recognized.

Around her, he barely recognized himself.

He wondered now what she thought of the sweater. Was it the right size? Would she like it? He hoped so. His only regret was that he hadn't been there this morning to see her eyes and smile.

ELLA WOKE UP to a nagging restless feeling. Boxing Day was a national holiday, and everyone would be gathering in the drawing room or library to spend more time together, but Ella felt trapped, and longed to do something... go somewhere... explore.

After lunch, she joined her sister who was planning to watch a holiday movie in the library with the aunts while Uncle Frederick and Alec were in Alec's study playing a game of chess. The movie, a romantic comedy set in England, was filled with a cast of superstar actors, but it was too sweet and charming for Ella's mood.

The last thing she wanted to watch was a half dozen people fall in love while she was trying to come to grips with how much she was missing Baird. After the movie ended, Aunt Emma and Dorothy went to put a tea tray together since Mrs. Johnson had the day off, and Ella sat down next to Cara on the leather couch. "I'm going crazy," she said lowly.

"I can tell," Cara answered, putting her arm around Ella's shoulders and drawing her close. "What can I do? How can I help?"

"Would you hate me if I wanted to go away for a few days?"

Cara turned a little to look Ella in the face. "You want to leave?"

"I was thinking about our earlier conversation and your suggestion that maybe I should take the train to Bath, just for the day. What do you think if I go this week?"

"I think it's a great idea. You'd love to see the Jane Austen museum, but why don't you stay for a night or two? Take one of those city tours, or a walking tour, because there is a lot to see."

"I don't want to abandon you though, Cara."

"You're not. I've got Alec here and I'd love for you to immerse yourself in the world of Jane."

Ella nodded, feeling a weight lift from her shoulders. She was excited to go explore Bath, and see all the places Jane wrote about in her books. "I'd be back way before New Year's Eve," she said.

"Do you know where you'd stay?"

"I don't. I'll look online this evening. I'm not sure if Alec has a part of town he thinks I should stay in. I won't have a car so obviously I'll be walking everywhere."

"Bath is a very walkable city, and if you stayed in the City Center, you'd easily be able to see everything. You'd also have time to do some shopping, have tea at the museum or in the café at the Assembly Rooms—"

"Or tea at both places."

"Even better." Cara smiled fondly at her sister. "I wish I could go with you."

"Next time," Ella assured her. "We'll take the twins—"

"Or leave them with Alec and we'll sneak away."

Alec entered the library just then. "What plans are you making that don't include me?"

Cara extended her arm to him, and he crossed the room and took her hand.

"Ella wants to go to Bath tomorrow," Cara explained. "I was lamenting I couldn't go, and we've agreed next time we'll make it a girls' trip. But I couldn't leave you."

"I wasn't worried," Alec said, lifting Cara's hand to his mouth and pressing a kiss to her palm before sitting down on the arm of the leather couch. "What advice have you given her?"

"I said she should talk to you." Cara smiled at Alec, her expression absolutely adoring. "You'd be able to advise her far better than me, although I do think she'd want to stay in Bath's City Center, don't you think?"

"Yes. You'll also want the eight twenty train in the morning," Alec said, turning to Ella. "That should get you the best connection and you'll arrive in Bath around one. I'll run you down the Bakewell station after breakfast."

"That would be wonderful," Ella said. "I'm looking forward to this."

"I'll find you a hotel," Alec added. "Some place convenient with a good restaurant so you don't have to go out at night if you don't want to."

"Thank you," Ella said warmly. She smiled from Alec to Cara. "You married a really good man, Cara. If I haven't said it before, I approve."

Cara laughed. "I did, didn't I?" And then she lifted her face for a kiss, and Alec obliged.

BAIRD SPENT THE afternoon at his aunt's house, playing the longest game of Scrabble of his life. He was glad when Kate finally won so he could take his leave. But once back in his flat, he paced around, and then poured himself a drink. But the whiskey didn't do the trick.

He was restless. Aggravated. He was happy he'd made his aunt happy, but nothing in his world felt settled or right.

Should he call Ella? Wish her a Happy Christmas?

Or should he wait and see if she would reach out to him?

Why had everything become so complicated?

He forced himself to sit in his leather armchair, legs on the ottoman and slowly sip his whiskey while he watched the fire. But the fire made him think of Ella, and he wondered if she was building a fire in the cottage hearth every day, or if it had burned out and she'd left it cold.

He wondered if she was plugging in the lights on the little tree.

He wondered if she was happy. He wasn't happy. One of them should be happy, and if he had to choose, it should be her.

Baird glared at the fire, the whiskey doing nothing to mellow him out. He hated feeling feelings. He hated them more than anything. This was exactly why Fiona had been a good fit. He was calm with her. He was disciplined and rational. He no longer felt rational.

Baird was still glowering at the fire when his phone rang. It was Alec calling to ask about Baird's plans for New Year's. Was Baird going to return, or was he planning on staying in Edinburgh?

"I'm not sure," Baird answered. "I haven't accomplished much this past week. I should stay here and try to get caught up."

"If you're sure, then I won't try to talk you out of it," Alec said. "But if you'd like to return before, Ella won't be here. She's taking the train to Bath in the morning and will be spending a few days there, returning for New Year's, so if you came now, you'd have the cottage all to yourself."

Baird set down his glass. "Who is she going with?"

"No one. She's traveling on her own. I've booked her a room near the Abbey. It's a nice place, and she'll be safe there. I put a call into the concierge and the staff will be keeping an eye on her."

"What train is she taking?"

"The one that leaves just after eight arriving around

one." Alec paused. "You're not thinking of meeting her in Bath, are you?"

Baird frowned at the phone. What a question. No, he wasn't thinking of meeting Ella in Bath.

He hesitated, his frown deepening, his frustration ratcheting.

Or maybe he was.

"Which hotel?" Baird asked, swearing he could feel Alex's smug smile across the line.

Alec gave him the hotel's name and address. "If you do go, and *if* you're getting along, could you drive her home for New Year's? She's not very confident about taking the train and I'd prefer Cara not to worry too much."

"This is why you called me," Baird said. "You called knowing I would go after her."

"I know you're attracted to her. I've known since the wedding. I don't know what happened to you two at the wedding, but something did, and whatever it was—is—it's still here. Maybe just face the facts—"

"Feelings are not facts."

"Okay, fine. But Baird, she would be good for you. You need someone like Ella, someone that makes you feel alive."

"I don't."

"You do. Baird, you're in danger of becoming a crotchety old man."

"Sounds like you've been talking to my Aunt Kate," Baird said grimly, hanging up on Alec.

He was not becoming a crotchety old man. And he wasn't cynical or bitter. People just needed to leave him alone.

NOT REALIZING HOW close the train station was to her hotel, Ella took a cab, but then on arriving was glad because she'd overpacked even if it was just a quick trip. She wasn't a smart packer. She had a tendency to always add a little more—one more blouse, one more pair of shoes—just in case.

After checking in, Ella headed out for a walk and late lunch thinking afterward she'd rest, not because she was down, but she wasn't really feeling good. Perhaps she was just tired after a few nights of not sleeping well. Perhaps reading might help, and some good chocolate. Chocolate and books improved everything.

She smiled at the doorman as he opened the door to her hotel and glanced toward the front desk and then the elevators.

Wait. What? Was that ... *Baird* ... in the lobby reading a newspaper?

Ella froze, trying to make sense of what she was seeing. It couldn't be him. Had to be a doppelganger. He was in Edinburgh, miles from Bath.

She started walking toward him, not sure what she felt, but it wasn't indifference.

He lowered his paper as she reached his side. "What are you doing here?" he asked.

It was Baird, all Baird. "What are *you* doing here?"

"I asked first," he said, folding his paper and rising. He kissed her cheek. "You look well, though."

"I'm in shock. How… When…"

"Just arrived," he said. "And you?"

"A couple hours ago, on the train." She just kept looking at him, unable to believe he was really, truly here. "But what brought you to Bath?"

"I came to see it."

It was the most ridiculous answer and yet his lovely deep voice, and that gorgeous accent of his, filled her with warmth. "You have a very close relationship with Bath then?"

"Not at all. I have no relationship with Bath, but that doesn't mean I can't remediate that. It's never too late to become a Bath aficionado."

She smiled, her first real smile in days. Everything had been dark and suddenly it was as if the sun was peeking out. She'd missed him far too much. "Well, I'm glad you decided to develop a relationship with Bath, and it's exciting that you decided to do it while I'm here. Perhaps we can explore a little bit of the city together." She looked at him hard, studying him intently. "That is, if we're still friends."

"If I can be friends with Bath, there's no reason I can't be friends with you." He held out his arm to her and she walked into the embrace. His head dipped, and he placed a kiss on her forehead. "You didn't like the pink sweater? The cardigan was too old fashioned for you?"

Ella wrapped her arm around his lean waist. Without all the bulky coats and sweaters, he was deliciously fit. Solid, hard, warm. And he smelled like heaven. "I love the pink cardigan. Pink is my favorite color. How did you pull that off?"

"I have my sources."

She laughed and held him tighter before reluctantly letting him go.

"It's actually not that complicated," he admitted, as she stepped back. "I called the shop, asked about a pink cardigan, and they had one, just one, so I thought I'd take a chance. I gave them my credit card and then I paid a courier to run it up to the house."

"I should have texted you, thanked you."

"Or called." His expression was impossible to read. "I didn't leave because of you. I sent Alec a text. I thought he'd tell you—"

"He did."

"My Aunt Kate needed someone to spend Christmas with, and so I made a midnight run to Edinburgh."

Which was exactly what Alec and Cara had told her, but Ella hadn't believed them. "I'm sorry for our argument on Christmas Eve."

"It's behind us," he said.

"Cara explained about the prenup to me. I understand it

better." She looked up at him, her gaze locking with his. "It doesn't mean I like it, but I understand it."

"A prenup is not romantic," he agreed.

"I'm not romantic," Ella protested.

Baird grimaced. "I'm not going to touch that one now. I've only just arrived."

"Probably smart," she agreed, glancing around the lobby and then back to Baird who had no luggage with him. "Are you staying here? Do you have a room?"

"I am, and I'm all checked in. I've just been hanging out here waiting for you."

"You could have texted." She couldn't risk poking him a little. "Or called."

"Yes, we have access to modern technology."

She looked up at him, and she smiled into his eyes, and she saw such warmth in his gaze that it filled her with hope. Maybe…

Maybe.

But she wouldn't let herself go there. It was too much too soon to imagine there could be a relationship. Baby steps were needed. First, a friendship, and then trust, and then perhaps deeper feelings could develop that would help them find a way.

BAIRD WAITED DOWNSTAIRS while Ella went to her room to

put on warmer more comfortable boots and to collect a knit cap and gloves. She didn't make him wait long. She was back down in just a few minutes and, while she bundled up, they discussed what they should do.

"What have you seen?" he asked.

Ella tugged her sage green knit cap on, pulling it down to her brow. "The train station. The outside of the Abbey. The front of the Pump House. I didn't go inside anywhere. I was just trying to get my bearings."

"What would you like to do first?"

"I was studying my map, and the Royal Crescent isn't far. Maybe a twenty-minute walk from here. What if we go there first, and then on the way back we could stop at the Bath Assembly Rooms and the Jane Austen Museum?"

It was good to see her, he thought. Really good to see her.

Baird had felt off the entire time he was home in Edinburgh, and he hadn't known why. But the heavy empty feeling was gone. He no longer felt low. It was amazing how just seeing her again lifted him, making the clouds part and the sun shine, despite the cold front moving in. "A sound plan."

She grinned and drew on her gloves. "I don't believe I've asked if you are an Austen fan."

"In the spirit of full disclosure, I wouldn't say I'm a fan, but I'm familiar with her work. My mother and sisters watched all the Austen BBC productions, and there were spirited conversations at home about Jane Austen versus Charlotte Bronte—"

"So, you know that Charlotte was not a fan of Jane Austen?"

"I do. My sister Allison, she's youngest of my three sisters, teaches English at a secondary school in Melbourne."

"That's who your parents are visiting?"

He nodded. "She'd love talking to you about books, but she'd probably be a little intimidated. Allison has a diploma in education, and she's working on her masters, so she's more than qualified to teach, but she doesn't have your education."

"You don't have to have a lot of degrees to be passionate about authors and reading." She followed him to the hotel entrance.

One of the doormen rushed to open the front door for them. Ella smiled and thanked the doorman as they stepped outside.

"Who do you like to read?" she asked Baird.

"I don't do much pleasure reading. I read so much for work that reading isn't my favorite way to relax."

"If you were to read to relax, who would you read?"

"Plato or Aristotle. Maybe Thomas Aquinas. Francis Bacon."

"Philosophers?"

"Philosophy of law. I'm always intrigued by the relationship between law and morality. We lawyers are focused on how law applies to a particular issue in a particular jurisdiction, but sometimes it's necessary to step back and remember the features of law shared across time, place, and culture."

"No wonder you don't enjoy reading anymore," she teased.

"I actually enjoy reading philosophy. I just don't make time to read, perhaps because I don't have much free time."

"Do you ever want more free time?"

That was an interesting question, and he didn't immediately answer. "A year ago, I would have said no, but now … maybe."

They had passed the Abbey and the crowded Roman Bath entrance. As Baird talked, Ella gestured for them to continue on Monmouth Place without needing to interrupt the conversation. But as they approached the Royal Theatre, Ella paused, touching Baird's arm.

"Oh, how could I have forgotten about the Royal Theatre?" Ella cried, stepping back to look up at the façade. "It's not the Theatre Royal, this one was built to replace that one, but both theaters were significant in Jane Austen's life, and society. The theater was one of the few places men and women could socialize. It was also one of the few places the different classes could mix. Jane would have been able to mingle and observe the aristocracy at the theater—" She broke off and laughed self-consciously. "But, of course, you know all of that. You're British and this is your history. I'm sure you were an excellent student, too."

"I held my own."

"Just like in a fight?"

He smiled at her. "You *are* bloodthirsty."

"I just like learning things about you. Tell me something I don't know. What was your favorite subject in school?"

"I was very strong in math, but I liked history best."

"Really?"

He nodded. "And science. Literature. I like literature."

"You've pretty much covered all the subjects."

"I did well in school."

"How well?"

He should be modest. He wasn't. "Very well. I was a King's Scholar."

"What is that?"

"It's one of fourteen awards granted each year at Eton. It's a significant award, covering all tuition and expenses, which is what allowed me to go there. We didn't have that kind of money, and I didn't come from that kind of family. No one in my family went to private schools, much less a school like Eton."

Ella heard the way he said Eton, as if it was a foreign thing, an almost painful thing, and she realized she knew nothing about Baird, his past, his work, his dreams. She'd always focused on that heat between them, that spark which defined so much of their interactions, but he was so much more than a ruggedly beautiful man. He had a life she knew nothing about and with her trip ending in a week, she'd never know.

But no, she wouldn't think that. She couldn't. She had to leave room for hope. "How did you win the award?"

"I took incredibly difficult tests. I'd never seen anything like it. I was sure I'd failed."

She put her arm around him, giving him a squeeze. "But you didn't."

"I didn't," he agreed.

"And that's where you met Alec."

"And now you know the rest of the story."

But it wasn't the rest of the story. There was so much story, and she wanted to know it all. Absolutely everything. Bittersweet emotion swept through her. There never was enough time for everything, was there?

"I do wish I'd planned my trip better." She glanced at the theater, smiling wistfully. "I would have loved to have come here to see a play, take a backstage tour. But I wasn't thinking about Bath. I wasn't thinking about anything when I bought my ticket to come. All I did was work until it was time to fly out and then I packed some clothes and got on the plane. Now I regret not being more organized."

"It sounds as if someone else just works and works and works," he said, taking her hand as they began to walk again.

"Touché."

"If you had more free time, what would you do?" he asked.

She thought about the question before answering, liking

how it felt, her hand in his. She felt warm, secure. "I'd travel. I'd read. I'd come see Cara and make sure the babies knew me. I'd want to be part of their lives, not be a stranger. But it is going to be hard with so much distance between us."

"Have you thought about looking for a teaching job in England?"

She hadn't. Ever. "I can't imagine a British university would want an American professor instructing students on British literature."

He shrugged. "But your dissertation isn't just on English authors. You're an expert on female authors of the eighteenth century, American as well as English. Cara has talked about your extensive research on Louisa May Alcott, and how you spent the summer before last at Harvard studying the Alcott papers. You had access to her original works and letters."

"I immersed myself in her world for months and I would have been perfectly happy being left there at the Houghton Library, with regular breaks to visit The Orchard House in Concord." She sighed, remembering. "I do love my authors and books. It's always been my happy place."

"Even after all these years?"

"The more I study, the more I appreciate how influential these women novelists were, and the changes they wrought on society. Their stories were entertaining, but they reflected society, and the woman's place within it. But they also shared the inner world, and a woman's hopes and dreams, all well as her intellectual capacity. Are there important female writers writing before Jane? Yes. But most of them were writing on spiritual matters, political matters, or stories with morals, focused on human failings resulting in tragedy. You couldn't escape human failings in Jane's work, but she also wrote stories that were hopeful, where love triumphs. Where happiness is essential. In the eighteenth century, women had such limited choices. They were not free to choose for themselves. They were utterly dependent on their fathers, their brothers, their guardians, and their future husbands—"

"Where have I heard that before? I could have sworn it was from an Austen movie, spoken by an Austen heroine."

"Probably Fanny Price. Mansfield Park." Ella stopped walking to face Baird. "MP is maybe my favorite Austen novel—"

"MP?"

"Mansfield Park," she clarified. "Obviously, I love them all, but Fanny, she's a fascinating heroine. A lot of Austen fans don't like Fanny, but I do. Shy, timid, raised in a horribly dysfunctional home, she's sent to her uncle's home where she's surrounded by people who do not love her, and continue to verbally abuse her. And considering what a harsh upbringing she had, she's still able to stand up to her uncle when he pressures her to accept Henry's proposal. The fact that she can stand up to him, the fact that she does, is proof of her growth and her inner strength. I find it remarkable that she could do that, and it's yet another reason why I respect Austen so much. Her heroines aren't perfect. They're complex and nuanced and as the reader, you want them redeemed. You want them to find their place in the world, but not just as a wife and mother, as a woman who is loved and respected. Valued. That is Austen's gift."

Ella exhaled hard, her heart thumping, pulse racing, her emotions stirred. "Oh dear, I've done it again. I'm a little too passionate about my work."

Baird smiled at her, his expression doing crazy things to her heart. "I know very few people who are truly passionate about their work. But not you. I like that about you."

"We should do what we feel strongly about. We should live full of passion. Gusto—" She broke off to add, "Those are writer Ray Bradbury's words, not mine. He always said a writer should write with zest and gusto. I believe people should live with zest and gusto. Life is short and precious. It's a gift and not to be wasted."

"You live by your heart."

"And you live by your head," she said.

"I do."

"So, I'm an oddity, all my zest and gusto."

"No. It's refreshing. I'm not sure how I'd feel about zest and gusto in the law firm, but when it comes to music and art, literature and science, the more zest and gusto the better."

She laughed, her emotions bubbling up, filling her with light and joy. Impulsively she gave his hand a squeeze. "I'm glad you are here, Baird. I'm glad you took the time to meet me. I was happy enough being in Bath on my own, but you have made it all so much better."

BAIRD LOOKED DOWN at Ella, her expression so alive, life and excitement radiating her. He'd never known anyone like her. Saying goodbye to her would be hard.

"I can call the theater later," he said, the vast gleaming Royal Crescent now visible. "See if there are any backstage tours this week, anything available."

She sucked in a breath, blue eyes huge. "You don't mind?"

It was the expression he'd wanted to see on Christmas, and he felt a pang in his chest, tender and tight all at the same time. "Of course not," he said gruffly. Especially not when she looked at him as if he were the greatest man alive, and he wished he could be that for her. He wished he was that kind of man.

But the years had changed Baird and his knowledge of the world had hardened him, making him callous, ruthless, selfish. Or so Fiona had claimed.

Was it true?

Was he really that much of a heartless bastard?

Chapter Eleven

It really had been the most wonderful day. A tremendous day, Ella thought, drawing a deep breath, so appreciative of it all.

They'd walked miles and toured museums—sometimes very slowly because Ella, who had to read everything, poured over each museum's brochure. They had tea twice, just because Ella loved it so much, and now after a late afternoon rest, they'd finally found a little place for dinner. It hadn't been easy getting in somewhere and so they finally went to the place that could get them in soonest, which proved to be a mistake.

It wasn't the best food, and it was terrible service, the waiter forgetting to take their order, and then forgetting to bring drinks, and then getting their order wrong, and then disappearing in the middle of their meal, never bringing the condiments Baird had requested for his potato.

But instead of ruining the night, their awful experience just made them laugh and compare their most memorable dining experiences, meaning, other bad ones.

From horrendous dining, they segued into religion and

faith. Ella told him she had faith. She was raised Methodist. Baird was raised in the Church of Scotland. Neither of them attended church regularly, although Ella definitely went more than Baird. She shared that she'd gone to a service on Sunday, Christmas Eve morning."

"I didn't know that," he said.

"You were at the house making your Eton Mess."

"It was a bit of a mess," he admitted.

"It was delicious."

"And the service on Sunday? Was it good?"

"It was. I needed it. I'm sure it won't surprise you, but you have this way of tangling me up in knots, and I needed some calm and perspective, and I don't know if I got a lot of perspective, but I left calm."

"That's something."

"I agree."

The waiter finally materialized with the bill, even though he'd forgotten to bring the dessert. Baird pointed to the missing dessert on the bill and asked to have it removed. The waiter didn't even apologize but he did disappear to get it corrected.

"Maybe we should get a recommendation from the hotel concierge about where we have dinner tomorrow night," Baird said.

Ella nodded emphatically. "That's a good idea."

"How about a drink at our hotel? They have a nice bar on the top floor."

"Nice."

It was a short walk back to the hotel and then a quick ride in the elevator. As the gleaming elevator doors opened, she could see across the dimly lit bar to the huge windows with an extraordinary view of Bath at night.

They found a low deep upholstered sofa near one of the windows and sat down. "What a view," Ella marveled, unable to look away from the stunning Abbey and the Roman Baths, illuminated by yellow light.

"The Pulteney Bridge," Baird added, gesturing to the covered bridge which had been inspired by Venice's Rialto Bridge. "I'll get drinks," Baird said. "What would you like?"

"What are you having?" she asked.

"Something I can sip."

Ella suddenly remembered how his mouth felt on hers, and it stirred the old longing. He had sipped her, tasted her, and she'd loved every minute of it. "I'll have the same."

He arched a dark eyebrow. "I'm having a whiskey. Get something you really want."

"I'm terrible at this. Order for me if you don't mind. Something you think I'd like."

His gold brown eyes met hers, held. "Challenge accepted."

"Wonderful. I've put myself in your hands."

If she hadn't been looking at him so closely, she would have missed the flare of heat in his eyes. But she had been looking and she saw the fire, and the desire reassured her. He wasn't indifferent to her. That spark between them, that powerful chemistry that drew them together in August, was still there. He might call it lust, but for her it was more. And maybe one day it'd be more for him, too.

Baird returned to their table with a port for her and a whiskey for him.

"No ice?" she asked, nodding to his drink as he sat down on the couch next to her.

He sat close, sitting the way a lover would. She liked it. And him. Very much.

"No. A whiskey nightcap should be neat, especially on a cold night."

"Does it taste different when it's cold?"

"It's not as bold and fiery. The ice reduces the heat, so it's a cooler, more controlled flavor."

"And you like the heat?"

Once again something sparked in his eyes. "Depends on the heat." He lifted his tumbler in a toast, his lips curving faintly, creases fanning at his golden eyes, so much like the color of his whiskey. "But I don't think that's a big surprise."

Her heart thumped, and her pulse raced. Her hand shook as she lifted her glass and sipped the port, pleased by the full, round sweet flavor and how it warmed her all the way down.

She held his hand as they enjoyed their nightcap. They didn't talk. They just sat close, no words necessary. Baird went for a second round and, when he returned, he stretched his arm around her shoulders, bringing her against his chest.

She wished time would just stop.

If only time could freeze right now with her feeling so good and secure. If only there were more of these perfect moments in life.

Eventually, they had to call it a night. Baird walked her to her room. They both stood there, neither speaking, the air heavy.

"Don't look at me that way," she whispered, drawing her key from her wallet.

"What way?"

"*That* way." It was hard to breathe, her pulse drumming, her legs ridiculously weak. "It's the way you looked at me in August, the way you looked at me earlier. It's not going to work. Not this time. I know you now. You shouldn't even bother."

HE SIMPLY SMILED. He also knew her now. "If that's the case, my look shouldn't bother you."

"But you know what you do to me. It's not fair."

"All day, I've wanted you. All night, I've wanted you. Even if nothing happens here, that doesn't change the fact that I want you."

"You want sex, and I want more."

"That is the worst oversimplification I have ever heard. I

don't want *sex*. I want *you*. And you say you want more, which I translate as you want love from me, not just sex."

"You have correctly interrupted everything."

She was maddening and yet he couldn't get enough of her. "Our desires aren't as different as you think. I want you. You want me. You want love. I know how to love."

"Love me, or… Love pasta? Love whiskey? This is so frustrating, and I hate futility."

He laughed.

She glared at him. "Do *not* laugh."

"I just thought it was cute, the way you said you hate futility. Made me wonder if there are people who enjoy futility."

"Please stop being so frustrating."

"What am I doing now?" he asked, voice dropping, expression warm.

"You're talking to me. You're looking at me. You're making me question everything, and I don't want to question anything. It's exhausting, and it's late."

"It is late, and I don't want you feeling so frustrated and confused. There's no need for confusion. What we have here isn't going to go away, and whether I come in your room or don't, tomorrow morning I will still want you as much as I do now. There's no getting you out of my system. It's too late for that."

"But if you come in. If we get … closer … I'll lose, not just my heart, but my self-esteem, and I can't have that. I can't do life, or love, your way. I can't just be squeezed into a corner of your life. I'd want so much more. I'd need so much more. I'd need ... everything."

HE SAID NOTHING, and she hurt on the inside, everything tender and raw. She wanted to launch herself at him and shake him or launch herself at him and kiss him until he broke and wanted her. Until he needed her. Closing the distance between them, Ella grabbed Baird by his coat lapels and stood on tiptoe to kiss him. The minute her lips touched his she felt a jolt of electricity. Heat flared, a lick of fire that brought everything fiercely to life.

This was what she had been waiting for, this was what she had been wanting.

His mouth felt achingly familiar, the pleasure just as intense as it had been in August. Kissing him was a relief. It took her out of her head and put her firmly in her body. She loved the pressure of his body, the firmness of his mouth, the scent of his skin, the hunger in his kiss.

He felt like home, felt like everything she loved and needed. But now that she'd found him, how was she just supposed to let him go? How was she supposed to forget his mouth, his taste, his kiss?

Ella ended the kiss and stepped back, crossing her arms tightly over her chest, trembling from head to toe. She shouldn't have done that, shouldn't have thrown caution to the wind. Every touch, every kiss, only added to the potential heartbreak. "I hope you're satisfied."

"You don't sound satisfied," he answered.

"I shouldn't have kissed you. It was a mistake."

"Why do those words sound familiar?"

"I hoped that by kissing you I would get you out of my system."

"Did it work?"

"No. It just makes me more frustrated with you."

"We can't have that," he answered reaching out to bring her close again, his arms wrapping around her, holding her firmly to his chest. "A frustrated Ella is very unhappy Ella."

She wanted to cry. There was no reason to cry. Nothing had changed. The world was exactly the same. "It's your fault. You are not supposed to be this attractive, not to me, not anymore."

His head dipped, his lips brushed her temple, between the arch of her eyebrow and her hairline. "I find you equally maddening," he said, brushing another kiss across her cheekbone. "All Christmas I thought of you. All Christmas I wished I was with you. I wasn't thinking of you naked, either. I wasn't thinking about sex. I was thinking about you, and how much I missed you, and how hard it will be when you leave."

Ella closed her eyes as his lips traveled along the jaw and then underneath her jaw. She sighed. "So, you care for a little bit for me."

"I do."

"And you'll miss me."

"Very much."

If that was supposed to make her feel better, it didn't. She took a deep breath, and gently eased away, trying to control the wild beating of her heart. "Will I see you in the morning?"

"Why wouldn't you?"

"I don't know. Sometimes you're just gone when I wake up."

His features tightened. "I'm not going anywhere. I'll be here in morning."

BAIRD DIDN'T SLEEP right away. It bothered him that she'd think he would just leave her, as if he was someone who routinely abandoned people. Baird did not abandon people. He'd never abandoned anyone. It surprised him that she didn't know that, or that she couldn't tell he was solid, he was dependable, he was trustworthy. He made a point of sticking with the truth, lies only destroyed trust. He learned early from his father, who was the most ethical man Baird knew, that a promise had to be a promise kept. He didn't bully, shame, or ridicule.

Baird switched to family law thinking he'd be able to

help people, that he'd be able to protect children and minimize trauma to families. It hadn't worked that way. Yes, there were cases where he could make a difference, but most of the time, the dissolution of a marriage involved pain, anger, and grief.

All of this weighed on him, and stayed with him, still very much on his mind as he met Ella for breakfast in the hotel restaurant. He must have made a sound as they were seated because Ella looked troubled. "That was a very heavy sigh, even for you," she said.

"Sorry. I've been thinking about work and the meetings waiting for me after the holidays."

"Tell me about your work."

He allowed a small smile. "You know what I do."

"You handle divorce cases."

"Amongst other things."

"Who are your clients?"

"Usually, high-profile people with a lot to lose."

"And they come to you?" she persisted.

"Yes. They come to me to protect their interests, and I do."

"Are they very wealthy then?"

"Most of them."

Her brows pulled. "And this is lucrative for you?"

"It can be. I'm expensive, and some of these cases drag on for months, if not years."

"If it is so lucrative, why do you hate it?"

So, she'd remembered what he'd said. He'd hoped that that particular conversation wouldn't stick, but it did. Baird thought of giving her a nonanswer, something superficial and easy, but for some reason he didn't have his guard as firmly in place as he should have. "Because there is little joy in representing people at the lowest point in their lives. They're angry, they're bitter, and they're ready to inflict the most damage possible on the other, regardless if it's a spouse or child."

"How horrendous," she said softly.

"It can be. Not all of the time, but there are cases I just want over. People I never want to see again."

She was silent a moment. "How do you keep it from impacting you?"

Baird was relieved to see the waiter approaching. "I'm not sure I have."

AFTER BREAKFAST, BAIRD arranged to have his car brought around to the hotel entrance. He'd asked the hotel concierge for some recommendations that would get them out of the City Center and Baird thought a morning excursion to Dyrham Park, a stunning late seventeenth-century house surrounded by formal gardens and ancient parkland, would be a good change.

"It's not Pemberley," Baird said as he parked, referencing

Chatsworth House which had been Jane Austen's inspiration for Mr. Darcy's home. "But the hotel concierge assured me Dyrham Park is worth a visit."

Ella knew Jane had visited Chatsworth in 1811 and stayed in Bakewell while writing *Pride and Prejudice*, and still hoped to see Chatsworth before she returned home. "Is Dyrham Park open today, or just the gardens?"

"It's all open today and tickets won't be a problem."

Because it was early and still quite cold, they toured the house first, and then went outside. A few people wandered around the formal gardens, but it was relatively quiet. Ella was happy to have escaped the crowds. She walked at Baird's side, content to just be silent. After the intense conversation last night, Ella still felt unsettled this morning.

"I don't know what you've been told about Fiona, but you are nothing like her," Baird said after a few minutes, the morning sun casting long fingers of light through the woods. "In the beginning, I thought it was a problem, but I realize it's a good thing. Fiona and I probably weren't the best match. We didn't have the connection you and I have. I didn't think it mattered, but in hindsight, we needed more chemistry. We needed stronger feelings."

She hadn't expected him to admit that. "If the feelings had been stronger, would you still be together?"

"Probably."

Another surprise. Ella processed this for a moment. "Would you have married her?"

"No." His voice was firm. "I still don't think marriage is right for everyone, and certainly not right for me."

"*Why?*"

"Because if you don't get married, you can't get divorced."

"Oh, Baird! How terribly simplistic."

"But true."

She looked at him, troubled. "I realize this is a huge leap, but I have to ask. And this isn't about Fiona anymore. This isn't about any other woman, or a hypothetical situation. This is about me. You and me. You're certain that even if one day you fell in love with me, you'd never marry me." She put up a hand to stop him, as if he was going to interrupt. "I realize that's jumping ahead a few steps, but it's something I need to know, before I kiss you again, or sleep with you, or anything else with you."

"That is a jump forward." He hesitated, seeming to struggle with his answer. "You can't see a future with me without a wedding ring?"

"It's not just a wedding ring. It's my dream to have a family, a career, and children. I can have both, and I want both."

He nodded slowly. "I understand."

They were at an impasse. She could feel it. He would not marry her. He didn't want children. It wasn't something he wanted or needed.

Ella swallowed hard, flattened but also strangely relieved.

She'd known that would be his answer, but she had to ask him, just in case. "I'm glad we talked," she said huskily. "Thank you for being honest with me."

Baird's phone pinged with a text. He ignored it, but it pinged again almost immediately.

"It might be important," she said, wanting a moment to gather her composure.

Baird drew his phone from his pocket and checked the messages. He exhaled hard.

"What is it?" Ella asked.

He glanced from the phone to her. "James Phelps has just been arrested for embezzlement. A lawyer from my firm just texted. It's all over the news."

Chapter Twelve

They returned to the hotel to pack their bags and head for Langley Park. They were silent for much of the drive to Bakewell, both concerned, both finding it easier not to speak.

As they neared the Peak District, Baird cleared his throat. "In light of the news, I'm going to stay at the house tonight. Alec needs to have legal representation in the event media shows up."

She nodded. "That's wise. I'm glad you're there for him. He's lucky to have you for a best friend."

Baird shot her a swift glance, surprised. "I didn't think you approved of how I've handled things."

"I didn't love the prenup, but I understand better now. Does it mean I like it? No. Does it mean I'll ever sign one? No. But you did what needed to be done." She exhaled, hating the butterflies flitting in her middle. "The closer we get to the house the more nervous I get."

"It's unsettling," Baird agreed. "But we'll feel better once we're there. Has Cara reached out to you?"

Ella smoothed the woolen fabric of her trousers over one

knee. "No. I take it you haven't heard from Alec."

"Nothing."

"Why do I feel like they're trying to protect us from this?"

"Alec does like to handle things on his own, his way, but this is going to get bigger before it fades away. But it will eventually fade away. News must be news, always dependent on fresh stories. Fortunately for Alec, something scandalous will happen somewhere and the attention shall shift." Baird reached over and took her hand, holding it firmly in his. "Don't look so worried. Alec isn't in trouble. He's going to be fine. Everything will be fine. I promise."

Ella nodded and held on to his hand tightly, grateful for his steadiness and comfort.

ARRIVING AT LANGLEY Park, Baird drove straight to the house and parked off the mudroom. Entering the house, they saw Mrs. Johnson in the kitchen.

"You'll find them in the library," the cook said.

Ella followed Baird through the house to the library, where it was just Alec and Cara. The aunts and Uncle Frederick returned home yesterday, and even though no one said it, Ella thought it had to be a bit of a relief that the older family members weren't present now.

"You're back early," Cara said, as Baird greeted Alec and

then leaned over to give her a kiss on the cheek.

"Bath was rather boring," Ella teased, taking a chair close to her sister's spot on the couch. "Especially in light of what might be happening here. Have any rude paparazzi shown up? Any calls I can help handle?"

"There have been a few calls," Cara said, smiling faintly, "but Mrs. Johnson is handling them. She doesn't tolerate any nonsense."

Mrs. Johnson entered with a tea tray then. "No, she doesn't," she said firmly. "I will not have my family pestered. Most of what's online now is click bait anyway."

Ella and Cara exchanged amused glances.

"I see you've made some of my favorite egg and cress sandwiches," Baird said.

"There are a few steak sandwiches in the mix as well," Mrs. Johnson said. "I didn't know if you'd had time for lunch, so hopefully this will hold you all over to dinner."

Ella hadn't felt hungry earlier but was starving now. "Thank you so much. I'm glad to be back." She looked at her sister and Alec. "I was worried about you two."

Alec shook his head. "There's no need to worry. There's nothing to be done. The word is out and whatever will happen will happen." He smiled, but it was strained. He looked tired but resolved. "We will get through. We always do."

ELLA WAS AT the cottage, curled up next to the fire and looking at the tree when she saw a sweep of headlights and then the headlights went off, and she heard voices and then the voices faded away. Whoever it was must have gone to the house.

A few minutes later, another car parked and more voices before those people too were gone.

Cars kept arriving, and finally, Ella threw on her pink sweater over her blouse and jeans, combed her hair, added a jacket and hurried up to the house to see what was going on.

A party was going on.

Ella stood in the doorway of the green drawing room, shocked. Baird joined her.

"What is happening?" she asked, seeing Cara in an armchair with women circled around her and Alec by the fireplace speaking with several men.

"These are neighbors," Baird said. "They've come to lend support."

The neighbors kept arriving, too, car after car, the doorbell ringing almost constantly. No sooner had the door closed than someone else was knocking, and Baird was there to open the door, pointing Alec's neighbors and friends into the green drawing room where everyone was gathering.

Ella had no idea who arranged the gathering, but someone had organized it, because everyone came with something—food, drink, flowers, gifts. They'd come to be there for Alec and Cara. They'd come to show support.

Ella could see from Alec's expression as he moved around the green drawing room that he was touched, and overwhelmed, by the display of friendship and solidarity. Perhaps Langley Investments would take a hit for being in the news, but Alec would make sure the company would recover. Alec wasn't egotistical. Alec never put business before friends or family. He valued relationships and this gathering at his house was proof that his community valued him every bit as much.

The gathering touched Ella's heart. Cara had wanted a party to create goodwill with the neighbors, but she hadn't needed to worry. The goodwill was there. Even better, Ella didn't hear one guest ask about Phelps, or the embezzlement. There was no mention of Langley Investments or business. But it didn't take the neighbors and friends long to see that Cara was expecting and, again, no one mentioned it until Alec stood by Cara, and with his hand on her shoulder, shared the news. The neighbors cheered, celebrating the announcement as good neighbors and friends do.

Ella was still smiling as the guests departed. Everyone was gone by ten, and after shooing Alec and Cara off, sending them to bed, Ella went around collecting glasses and plates, crumpled napkins, tidying things so Mrs. Booth and Mrs. Johnson wouldn't have to tomorrow.

Ella was quite happy to be in the kitchen on her own. The plates had been scraped and were soaking in hot soapy water. The crystal had been rinsed and was waiting to be washed next. She spread dishtowels all over the marble counter and then began to wash, enjoying the ritual of washing, rinsing, and setting on the towel to drain and dry.

Baird entered the kitchen. He'd changed into sweatpants and a thick shirt. "I've come to work," he said, pushing up his shirt sleeves.

"There's nothing for you to do," she answered. "I've got this all under control."

"It meant a lot to Alec, seeing everyone show up here," Baird said taking a dish towel from a drawer and helping her anyway. "I think it was good for him to see how much he matters to people."

"I was thinking the same thing. He looked happy, didn't he?"

Baird nodded. "Cara looked happy as well."

Ella picked up a dish towel and began buffing the crystal stemware dry. "I hadn't expected the baby announcement tonight. But Cara can't hide the bump anymore."

"I think it was a good thing. It will just make the community even more protective of them."

"Were you the one who suggested Alec share the news?"

Baird reached for another dessert plate. "No. I would have counseled against it. But in the end, I think it was fine."

"Why would you have recommended against it?"

"I don't like children being in the middle of things. I hate to see them exposed to social media. I hate it when adults make money off of them. It's exploitive."

Ella paused and looked at him, really looked at him. "You're going to be a wonderful godfather to the twins."

He looked embarrassed and said nothing. But once the dishes were done and the counters had been wiped down and dish towels hung up to dry, he filled the kettle with water. "Will you have a cup with me?"

She nodded and pulled out a counter stool and sat down, watching as Baird set out a teapot and two teacups. He opened one of Mrs. Johnson's baking tins, filling a dessert plate with ginger cookies and shortbread. When the water boiled, he let it sit for a little bit before he poured the hot water over the loose tea leaves. While the tea steeped, he carried the sugar and milk to the counter, along with spoons and a tea strainer.

Once everything was ready, he brought the teapot and teacups to the counter and then sat down next to Ella.

They drank their tea and said not much of anything and then as the cookies disappeared and their tea was almost gone, Baird moved his cup back and looked at her. "I've already told Alec that I'm heading back to Edinburgh in the morning, so I'll be back home for New Year's Eve."

She should have expected it, should have been prepared, but she wasn't. He was leaving again? "When tomorrow?"

"Probably early."

She said nothing. She dropped her head and fought a wave of intense emotion—sadness and disappointment and regret.

He put a hand out and covered her knee. "I don't live here, Ella. This isn't my home, and I've never spent this much time at Langley Park. I need to go."

She nodded, not trusting herself to speak.

"It will probably be quiet here, but it'll be good for everyone. You and Cara will be able to spend some quality time together, too."

Ella again nodded, and blinked, fighting to hold back the emotions that were sweeping through her. She would miss him. She didn't know when she'd see him again. She'd dreaded the goodbye, but it was coming so much sooner than she'd imagined.

"You have plans for New Year's," she said, trying to make her voice strong but she still didn't know where to focus, afraid that if she looked into his eyes, she'd lose her composure entirely.

"There are always plans for New Year's, but you're only here until early next week and then you're back to Washington and your work there." He hesitated. "I hope we're parting on good terms. It was difficult last summer and hard on both of us."

"Was it hard on you?" She glanced up into his face and his warm gold eyes.

"Very hard. You know I care about you."

"Even then?"

"Yes, Ella," he said, taking her hand. "Even then. I've never left you and thought oh, great, this is a good thing.

That's not how I feel, and that's not how it works."

She searched his eyes. "If I didn't want a family, would you want me?"

"Ella, I want you now. But knowing how important having a family is to you, I can't in good conscience pursue a relationship with you. There's no future for us."

She loved the feel of his hand against hers, his skin so warm, his palm slightly calloused. "Well, there is a future, but it sounds awfully painful because at some point we'd be fighting and saying goodbye."

"Precisely." His fingers curled around hers. "It's hard enough saying goodbye to you now. I can't imagine how it'd feel in six months, or six years. I don't know that I could do it."

"So, we cut the cord while we can." Ella drew her hand from his and forced a smile, but her insides burned raw, as raw as if she'd scraped something sharp.

"Do you have a better solution?"

"We go with it. We try it. We see how we feel."

He sighed. "Where's the logic in that?"

"Love isn't logical, but it's real, and its important and it shouldn't be thrown away just because we might want different things in the future. The future isn't here. The future you're afraid of might never come."

"And what future would that be?" he asked, getting off his stool to go lean against a counter, arms folded across his chest.

"It's just so … obvious … you're operating from a place of fear, not confidence. If you were confident, Baird, you wouldn't need to be afraid of relationships, or falling in love."

"I'm not afraid of falling in love."

"You're afraid of being hurt, of being left, and so you end things before others can, because you expect to be hurt—"

"I've never been hurt," he interrupted. "Fi never hurt me. We didn't have that kind of relationship. It wasn't dramatic. It certainly wasn't loud or unpredictable. We were very close."

"Then how could you possibly let her go?" Ella looked at him, expression fierce. "Either you didn't love her deeply, or you were afraid to risk loving her more, and so rather than marry and truly commit, you let her go."

He growled impatiently. "In case you've forgotten, you're earning a PhD in eighteenth-century literature, not psychology. I've never been crushed by a relationship, nor have I had my heart broken. I'm glad you find me so fascinating, but your theories aren't based in reality."

"In that case, I feel better. I'm glad you weren't hurt, because it sucks. It feels awful. And I'm glad you're not using all the divorce cases you handle as reinforcement. I'm glad that every time you feel strongly, you don't remind yourself that love becomes a weapon, and you protect yourself from that danger by not falling in love and not letting others get too close to you."

His brow furrowed deeply. "I'm glad you are glad.," he said grimly.

"Me, too. I'm glad you come from a family without divorces. I'm glad I come from a family without divorces. I'm glad you have proof that not everyone ends up divorced and cruelly fighting over assets and children. I'm glad you also know you use excuses to protect yourself, no matter how much it hurts others. As long as you're not having to take any risks or expose yourself to pain, you're in good shape."

"I've never liked your sarcasm. Have I told you that before?"

"A couple times."

He pushed off from the counter. "I think it's time we said good night and goodbye before this turns ugly.

Ella slid off her stool, hands on her hips, blocking his path. "It's already ugly, Baird. I'm livid. Livid with you."

"I know you're disappointed—"

"Yes. Disappointed, furious, heartbroken, disgusted. You show up for everyone but you. You put everyone else's needs before your own—"

"That's not true. We've just established I'm selfish and putting my needs first."

"You aren't selfish. You are always there for Alec. You are there for your family—you drove home at midnight on Christmas Eve for your Aunt Kate. You are there for your firm, you are there for your clients, but when are you there for yourself?"

He tried to step around her, but Ella just blocked him again.

"How am I not there for myself?"

"You've created a lot of rules about love and commitment, rules for your future, and these rules are to protect you, so you don't get hurt, and you don't have to take risks, rules that ultimately give you the upper hand in relationships. In short, you work very hard to maintain control, but the control means you don't get to really feel. Or love. Or be loved in return."

Baird was not smiling. "You're upset because I've decided not to pursue a relationship with you."

"Because it's the easiest thing to do. It's easy walking away from people. The hard thing is sticking around and showing up and learning how to make love and life work. You and I could make it work, but it's a choice, and it's a choice we'd have to make every day."

He said nothing, his expression shuttered closed.

"By the way," she added, taking a step toward him and pointing a finger at his chest, "I looked up UK divorce statistics and Scotland has a lower divorce rate than England, and it crossed my mind that the divorces you handle, those divorces which had made such a big impression on you, aren't the norm but more representative of the very wealthy who love and protect their things more than other people." Her chin jerked up. "Maybe the ugliness is due more to a personality type than the population in general."

"So, now I've become your research paper."

"No, but I am trying to make sense of it. To make sense of you. I just don't understand why someone like you, someone who is successful and kind and apparently well-adjusted, would be so incredibly negative about marriage and family, the very thing that brings most people meaning and joy."

"Stop analyzing me. Stop overthinking. It's not helping, and you're just going to ruin whatever is left of us. Stop while we have some good memories—"

She laughed. "I have a feeling you said the same thing to Fiona." She took a step back and then another one. "I imagine you were very calm and centered. Mr. Mature letting his love of many years go. Did you open the door for her, or just close it after she was gone?"

"I'm not going to do this." Baird stepped around her, avoiding making any contact with her. "I'm sorry you're upset. I'm sorry you're disappointed. I appreciate that you're passionate and emotional, but it's a little unhinged—"

"Unhinged?" she cried. "I'm not allowed to feel deeply? To grieve that something that could be wonderful is ending?"

"Feelings this strong can't be good. Not for me."

"Did none of your sisters ever cry? Did they never have a broken heart? Did you treat them scornfully then?"

"You're tired. It's late."

"Do not, Baird, do not patronize me. Do not mansplain love to me, especially when you don't know what love is."

He stepped into her space, towering over her. "I know what love is. But this … this isn't love. This is…" He shook his head, voice drifting away. "This isn't right. This isn't healthy, or mature love. Fiona and I had a mature relationship—"

"*Please*. Don't say that you had a mature relationship. It doesn't sound mature, it sounds empty and cold. I would never be satisfied with a quiet, mature relationship. I want mad-crazy passion."

"Obviously. It fits the mad-crazy part of you."

"You're right. I'm mad crazy right now. I'm mad crazy for you. I'm mad crazy fighting for you. I refuse to let you go without a fight. I refuse to just wave you off and act as if you don't mean more to me than any other man I've ever met."

He said nothing and she knew her mad crazy had just scared him off. If he hadn't already been done, he was certainly over it—and her—now.

She sniffled, holding tears back. "I think love should be passionate. I think desire should be strong. Which is why I'm glad Fiona gave you an ultimatum, and I'm glad you set her free. Fiona deserved more from you. She deserved all of your heart. She deserved to be swept off her feet, and to have you make her feel like the most wonderful woman in the world, and if you couldn't do that, you were the wrong man for her."

"We've already agreed on that."

"Then let's also agree that love should be a positive. Love should be big and inspiring, full of hope and wonder, as well as courage and conviction. You should love someone so much that you will spend the rest of your life fighting to protect that love, and fighting for the best for the person you love." She moved close, put her hand on his chest, her palm pressed over his heart. "Baird, if it's your work in family law that has made you mistrust people, then you should get a different job. If your work has made you cynical, your work is terrible for you. No matter how much you earn."

Ella dropped her hand and took several steps back, shoving her hands into her jean pockets to keep from touching him again. "I'm glad we had tea tonight. I'm glad you told me you were leaving. And as brutal as it was, I'm glad we had this talk. I understand everything so much better, and why you can't care for me—"

"I *do* care for you," he snapped.

"But not enough. Not that way I want to be loved. And if I'd known all this back in August, I wouldn't have hurt as much. I would have realized you weren't the one for me. I would have realized that while kissing you was fun, you're not good for my heart, and you're not good for my head."

She took another step back, her voice cracking. "The next time I love someone, it's going to be someone who will let me be me, full of mad-crazy love. And I hope for you that you find your perfect woman and you love her and, once you love her, she breaks your heart just a little bit."

"Why?" he demanded.

"Not all the way. Just enough for you to realize that love is precious, and life is short, and we can never take either for granted."

ELLA NEEDED AIR. She needed space.

She walked quickly to the mudroom and grabbed her coat on the way out the door.

It had begun to snow. She stopped and just looked up. The snow was falling silently, thickly, large white flakes tumbling from the sky.

It was beautiful, it was painful. She'd been wanting snow since she'd arrived and now it was here. Snow falling, covering everything in white.

Her heart hurt. She hurt. She couldn't do this with Baird anymore.

She couldn't try anymore, hope anymore, give anymore. She couldn't want him when he didn't need her love. She couldn't need him when he didn't love her in return.

She walked and then stopped, fighting tears. How magical it all was, the woods dusted in white, snow piling on branches, frosting the ground.

Everything about Langley Park was a fairytale, except for the part where you get your heart broken. She held out a bare hand, caught snow and watched it cling to her fingertips before it began to melt.

Ella blinked back tears. She wasn't going to fall apart. She wasn't going to cry. There was no point in crying. It was time to let go. No more hoping and wishing. It was just too painful. She walked toward the cottage, brushing snow from her face. Instead of stopping at the cottage, she kept going, walking on to the dairy, which had been turned into an event venue. It hadn't been booked out for New Year's Eve but would be booked next Saturday for a wedding. Ella circled the dairy, and then walked back to the cottage, cold. Frozen.

Don't think.
Don't think.
Don't feel.

BAIRD WAS ANGRY when Ella walked out. He was angry and raging on the inside because she didn't know him. She didn't know who he was or what he wanted and for her to think her wildly arrogant lecture was a sign of maturity, well, she was wrong.

So wrong.

But Baird hadn't even made it up a flight of stairs before he felt remorse and guilty. She'd been the one to turn everything upside down and inside out, but he cared about her enough not to want her returning to the cottage so hurt and upset. He wasn't rejecting her. He wasn't punishing her, and he didn't like to think of her being alone in the cottage, crying. Normally, tears didn't move him, but it was different when Ella cried.

When her eyes welled up, they looked even more like the sea, and she was the Ella at the reception, the one he hadn't met, the one who reminded him of a woodland fairy—beautiful and bright and impossibly alive.

Suppressing a groan, he turned on the staircase and went back down. He didn't chase jobs, he didn't chase people, he didn't chase women, but he was going after Ella. Not to have the last word, but to make sure she was okay and not crying her eyes out.

Stepping outside though, he discovered it was snowing and the snow was a huge surprise.

The wind was blowing, too, making the snow swirl and vision difficult. Baird had been coming here for years so he knew his way, but there were moments he had to pause and make sure he was still heading the right way.

Baird reached the cottage and knocked the snow off his shoes before opening the door and going inside. But the downstairs was dark, and there were no lights on anywhere. He climbed the stairs and checked her room. It was empty, the bed made. She wasn't here.

He stood in the upstairs hall, trying to figure out his next move. He'd go check the dairy. Perhaps she'd gotten lost and ended up there. It would have been easier if there had been footsteps to follow but the snow had already covered them up.

Baird returned outside, walked down the white road, his footsteps the only ones he could see. The dairy doors were locked. He walked all the way around the brick building. No sign of Ella.

Baird checked his watch. It was midnight and cold. He tried to picture where Ella might have gone, but he was coming up blank. Had Ella maybe returned to the house? But wouldn't Baird have seen her?

Baird didn't want to alarm Cara, but Alec needed to know. It was freezing outside, and Ella couldn't be out wandering around on her own, not in a snowstorm, not anytime. She had to be found, and she had to be found now.

Alec answered Baird's call immediately.

Baird wasted no time. "Ella left the house tonight upset, I went to check on her, but she isn't in the cabin and it's snowing. I can't find her."

"Where are you now? Alec asked.

"Back up at the house, outside, going around to check all the doors. Just in case."

"I'll meet you downstairs."

They spent the next thirty minutes walking, searching, shining flashlights across the woods, the vast front lawn, and down toward the cottages where they checked every door and front steps.

"She wouldn't have gone to Bakewell," Alec said. "She's got to be at the house. Maybe we just missed her somehow."

Baird nodded but said nothing. He felt sick, heartsick. He didn't know if this was his fault, but he did know he was afraid for her, and he'd never felt fear like this for anyone before.

He didn't know why she'd take off in the snow. It made no sense to him, and even if she was a hothead, she wasn't irresponsible, and she'd never risk her safety to prove a point. She was missing because something had happened, and that something filled him with fear.

At the house, they checked all the downstairs rooms, from the green drawing room to Alec's personal study. While Alec checked the family wing, Baird went back to the kitchen, the walk-in pantry, and Uncle Frederick's suite.

Alec returned downstairs. "Let's head back out, and if we can't find her soon, I'm going to call the police and ask for help."

"Let's go back to the cottage once more," Baird said. "See if her things are all there, or if she's packed or taken anything. I can't imagine where she'd go at this time of night, but we have to find her. I will find her."

The cottage was still dark. The downstairs was cold. Upstairs, Ella's room was still empty, her bed still made. Alec checked the first bedroom then. Baird checked the next.

And then Alec said quietly, "Baird, she's here."

"Where?"

"Here. Isn't this your old room?"

Baird squeezed past Alec to look into his room, and yes, she was there, curled up in his bed, the covers tucked beneath her chin.

Relief flooded Baird, relief and gratitude and something else so deep and profound that he couldn't even articulate it. "Why is she in here and not her room?" he asked, voice low.

Alec clapped Baird on the should. "I'm going back to the house." He gave Baird a look. "I'm not going to tell you what to do, but it would be a great deal easier on my marriage if you do not have to break Ella's heart."

"The last thing I want to do is break her heart," Baird said, voice rough.

He didn't want to hurt her. He loved her. He wanted more time with her. If it was possible, he wanted forever with her. He didn't want Ella finding forever with anyone else. He didn't want someone wooing her and winning her and making all her dreams come true. That was his job. That was what he wanted to do.

"I'll see you in the morning," Baird said.

Alec paused at the end of the hallway. "I thought you were leaving."

"It doesn't make sense to rush out early now. But thank you for coming to help me find her. I appreciate it."

"You did the right thing calling me. I'm just glad she is safe. Good night."

Alec left, and Baird stood in the doorway several long

minutes watching Ella sleep.

He didn't know why she climbed into his bed, in his room. He certainly hadn't thought to look for her here but at least she wasn't outside in the snow, lost, scared, ranting about mad-crazy love.

His jaw eased and he smiled faintly. He'd fallen for the most illogical woman he'd ever known. He didn't know what would happen next, he just knew leaving her wasn't the right decision. Letting her go wasn't right, either.

He'd never fought for a relationship before because he didn't think one was supposed to fight for a relationship. It either worked or it didn't. It was supposed to be clear and simple. Straightforward as well.

But maybe when you met the right person your perspective shifted, and you were willing to consider things you'd never considered before.

He wasn't ready for marriage and children—far from that—but he could see that his hard, fast rules were problematic. Love meant opening your mind not just your heart.

Baird slid his coat off and placed it across the chair in the corner. He then sat down on the foot of the bed and eased his boots off.

Maybe you knew you'd met the right person when you suddenly felt a little mad crazy yourself. When your emotions weren't tidy and easily controlled.

Maybe you knew it was love because you realized that you were not going to live without it. Not if you could help it. Not if you could fight for it.

Baird eased his wool sweater off, drawing it over his head and then removed his heavy belt before climbing onto the bed, and lying close to Ella, one arm around her waist, to keep her safe.

She smelled like cinnamon and snow and love. He held her a little tighter. No one had ever gone toe-to-toe with him before. No woman had ever gotten in his face, much less said the things Ella said to him tonight. But he was glad she did, and he was glad he'd been angry, or he wouldn't have gone after her, and he wouldn't have realized how much he loved her and refused to lose her. Until the moment when she seemed lost, he'd been focused on his anger, but once he couldn't find her anywhere, his anger shifted into something entirely different, into something that was nothing to do with him, but her.

She had to be safe. She had to be okay. She had to be found. He couldn't bear the thought that she was hurt, or in pain, or lost somewhere in the snow.

And he would find her. He had to find her. She was his and he loved her and every thing in him was focused on finding her, saving her, and loving her. Forever. Baird had never had such clarity. He had one purpose and one purpose only—bring her home.

Ella murmured something and he kissed the top of her head and closed his eyes. It was late. He was exhausted. But for the first time in months, he felt peace. That clarity during the search had give him insight into his heart. He did love, and he loved his Ella immensely. He could lose everything but her.

They were going to work this out. They could work this out. There was no way he'd let the best thing that had ever happened to him just go without a fight.

ELLA WOKE WARM, a little too warm. She stretched and bumped into something very big and solid next to her. Opening her eyes, she discovered Baird in bed with her. He was still dressed, but he was under the covers, sound asleep, looking a little bit like an angel, which wasn't fair considering how he'd been anything but an angel last night.

But he was here, and that was good.

Very good.

She was glad he hadn't gone yet. She'd fallen asleep hating herself for all the things she'd said to him. She'd been hard and harsh, and she hadn't held back. She'd been like a street fighter, throwing everything at him, giving him everything she had. Okay, she'd been a little unhinged, but she was panicked and desperate and couldn't bear losing him.

She'd been certain she'd said far too much.

She'd been certain she'd made him hate her—Baird intensely disliked strong emotions—but somehow, through some miracle, he was here, with her, holding her as if he'd never let her go.

She realized he'd opened his eyes and was looking at her. He didn't look sleepy or confused.

"Hi," she said, insides fluttering because he really was the most beautiful man she'd ever known. "What are you doing here? You were supposed to stay at the house and then leave early."

"I know, but I was worried about you last night. So I went to find you and then I couldn't find you and I called Alec and after quite a long search, he discovered you in here, safe in this bed." Baird's expression was rueful. "I never thought to check this room. It probably would've saved a lot of walking in the snow."

"You didn't have to come after me. I wasn't very … sensitive … last night."

He smiled crookedly. "No, you weren't. But then I think we both know you're a bloodthirsty wench." He paused. "I mean that in the nicest way."

She tried to smile but couldn't. "What time are you leaving?" she asked, reaching out to touch his jaw.

"I don't know. We'll have to talk about that later, after we sleep some more."

Ella snuggled closer. "Deal."

A PHONE RANG at ten and Baird groped around the bed trying to find it.

"It's me," Ella said sleepily, finding her phone on the nightstand. "Hi, Cara. No, everything's good. Just, um, sleeping in. Don't apologize, everything's good. Thank you. Bye." She said goodbye and hung up and, yawning, pressed her cheek to Baird's chest.

"Mrs. Johnson is sending a hot breakfast down to us since we missed breakfast at the house."

"Does that mean we have to get up?" Baird asked, rolling onto his back and dragging a hand through his thick hair, disheveling it further.

"You only have to get up to make me coffee and then you can go back to bed," Ella said, leaning over him to kiss him.

He caught the back of her head and brought her mouth back down to his. He kissed her hard. "You scared me to death last night. I thought I'd lost you."

She looked down into his eyes, and his normally gold eyes were dark and shadowed. "I'm sorry. I didn't think you'd come looking for me and I wasn't trying to hide from you."

"Why were you in here and not your room?"

She hesitated before whispering, "I wanted to feel close to you."

Baird wrapped his arms around her and held her to him tightly. "We have a lot to discuss, but how about some coffee first?"

"I would very much appreciate that."

The second pour-over coffee was nearly done when one of the estate staff showed up with a hot breakfast in a dozen different dishes. Baird began immediately serving the breakfast, and it was one of those huge English breakfasts with eggs, bacon, mushrooms, tomatoes, beans, and piles of toast."

They ate facing each other at the rustic table, the Christmas lights on the tree plugged in, and the fire crackling in the hearth. They focused on eating until they started slowing down. Finally, Ella stopped eating to just concentrate on her coffee.

"I have a thought," Baird said, spreading some of Mrs. Johnson's homemade marmalade on another triangle of toast. "What if we take away the rules—my rules—and your expectations. What if we decide we're not going to make any big decisions until you're done with your PhD, and then this summer we can figure out what's best for us, whether that's me going to the States, or you coming to the UK?"

Ella's hand wobbled as she set her coffee down. "I'm a little lost," she said, voice catching. "Last night—"

"Was an enormous wake-up call. I was so afraid we weren't going to find you and it scared me, Ella. It made me physically sick. I can't picture a future without you. I don't want a future without you. I want what Alec and Cara have. I want you. I want love. I want us."

Ella sat there gaping at him, speechless. She couldn't think of a single intelligent thing to say.

"I realize I can be a little black and white," Baird added. "So, I propose a little bit of gray. I propose we not make decisions we don't have to make, and perhaps we just like each other, and enjoy each other, and see where that takes us."

"What if we discover we still like each other? What if we end up deliriously happy? Won't that be a problem?"

"Not if we're happy," he said.

She wasn't satisfied with that. "Baird, if I love you the way I want to love you, I will want everything with you. I'll want little MacLaurens with you. I'll want noise and chaos. I'll want all the things you don't."

"What do you think I want?"

"A clean, tidy ultra-organized home without the pitter-patter of little feet and the sound of children fighting."

"You are so dramatic, Ella. Why would you think I want an ultra-organized home? Couldn't an organized home be good enough?"

"You know what I'm saying. I'm intense and passionate, and that's not for you."

"I think I was wrong. I think I must crave a little intensity, because last night when I couldn't find you after searching the woods, and checking the field, and going to each of the cottages, searching for footsteps, searching for any sign of you, I realized I'm not going to live without you.

It's not an option. I want you. I want to be with you. And if we can make this work, why don't we try?"

"Baird, I can be happy with you without a marriage license. It's not a wedding I want. It's you. But being a mom? That is important to me. I love my family. I love the closeness and the traditions and just feeling as if I'm part of something bigger than me, something more important than me. And if I continue to love you, I will want all of that with you."

"I understand. I do. Which is why I propose we don't make hard decisions today. Why not just give us time? Why not just … be happy … and see where that takes us?"

For a moment, neither said anything and then Ella slowly nodded. "Happy with you is something I can do." She smiled, eyes watering. "And I agree there is no reason to make hard and fast decisions today. Let's just be happy today."

"I was hoping you'd say that." He reached across the table for her hand. "Want to come to Edinburgh with me for New Year's? I'd love to show you my city and where I live."

Ella started smiling, and her smile just got bigger. "Really, seriously?"

He laced his fingers between hers. "I know you have school starting in a couple of weeks, but June will be here before we know it, and we might as well have fun and explore our options, realizing we can do whatever we want to, whenever we want to."

The air caught in her throat and for a moment Ella couldn't breathe, and then she rose up and leaned across the table to kiss Baird, and once she began kissing him, she couldn't quit. But then she had to if only to tell him how much she loved him. "I'm crazy about you."

"I know. I saw the crazy last night," he teased and then he came around the table and scooped her up into his arms and carried her into the living room where he sat down on the couch with her on his lap. "But I'm glad because you were right. I have been afraid. I don't want to risk everything and then be hurt."

She traced his lovely cheekbone and then his jaw. "I won't hurt you."

"But even if that happens, it's worth the risk. You have no idea how much I love you, and how much I want you. I discovered just how much I believe in us."

She clasped his face between her hands and smiled into his eyes. "I believe in us, too. I believe we are going to have the most wonderful life together—with kids, without kids. The point is that we will find a way together, and together we become a family."

He held her against him. "Together we're home."

Ella didn't think she'd ever heard anything so lovely in all her life but then another thought came, and she sat back up, excited. "So, when do we go to Edinburgh?"

He smoothed her hair back from her brow. "When do you want to go?"

"Today?"

Baird kissed her until she couldn't think straight, and then, and only then, he lifted his head. "Today it is."

She grinned at him. "I can't wait. Happy everything, Baird."

"Happy everything, my Eloise."

Epilogue

Everyone that could come, did, traveling in for the late July christening of baby Viscount William Frederick Sherbourne, and his twin, Lady Emma Eloise Sherbourne, younger by two minutes, but twice as feisty as her good natured older brother.

Baird was selected to be the godfather for little William, and Ella was asked to be Emma's godmother, as she was also her—partial—namesake.

The three month old babies were healthy and active, and besotted with each other, always reaching out to take the other twin's hand or to press open mouth kisses on each other's faces and head. William had a few wisps of brown hair but Lady Emma was completely bald with the palest skin and the roundest head. Some of the Roberts family were already speculating that delicate Emma might end up a redhead, but regardless of her coloring, Emma and William were adorable together, and never lacked attention, always arms there to scoop them up and take them for walks, even if it was just around the house on a stormy day.

Baird was one of those constantly carrying the babies,

humming to them or crooning a Gaelic ballad which inevitably made Ella's eyes sting and tear up. There was nothing she loved more than to hear him sing, which usually meant catching him when he was alone because he was too shy to sing before an audience. But Baird was happy, happier than she'd ever known him. He'd left family law and was focusing on corporate law again but with a focus on corporate ethics and morality, specifically the role corporations played in society and their responsibility to society. He was earning substantially less but believed in what he was doing, and felt as if he was finally giving back in a way that made him proud.

She was proud of him, so pleased that he'd arrived in Derbyshire the day after the babies arrived to meet them, sending Ella and the Roberts family endless videos and photos of the new arrivals and Cara who looked radiant with her tiny bundles of joy. While Ella hated not being there herself as she was nearing the end of the teaching semester, and finishing her dissertation, but the moment she was done, she flew out of Seattle into Edinburgh.

After spending a few days with Baird they drove down to Langley Park to meet the newest Sherbournes. The rest of the Roberts family that could manage time off and the flights, arrived in July to spend a week at Langley Park and be present for the baptism and the summer party Alec and Cara was hosting today on the lawn.

Ella sat with Cara now in the shade of a tree and watched

the games, each of them holding a baby while Baird and Alec taught the visiting Americans how to play cricket.

"Your anniversary is coming up in less than a month," Ella said to Cara, adjusting little Emma in her arms. "Are you and Alec making any plans?"

Cara glanced down at William, his small mouth pressed to her chest. "We'll probably have dinner here, just a small celebration for us. Mrs. Johnson promised to make something special because she knows I don't want to go anywhere, and Alec won't. He doesn't want to let the children out of his sight. There are so many nights I wake up and find him in the nursery just keeping watch." Her lips curved. "He's such an amazing father. I'm so lucky."

"You are," Ella agreed, even as she looked out to the lawn where Baird was showing Ethan, one of her brother Tom's boys, how to hold the bat.

She felt lucky, too, lucky to have found a man she loved dearly, completely, with all her heart, a man who loved her just the same. With her degree behind her, and the future ahead, she felt excitement but also peace. She and Baird had found each other and it worked. All the pieces fit. She flashed back to Christmas and the puzzle they'd worked on in the green drawing room, the one of the Highland cows looking over the stone wall.

Sometimes life was like a jig saw puzzle. It didn't always come together easily, and sometimes breaks were needed, and sometimes pieces went missing and sometimes you tried to force a piece into the wrong place and it didn't work. But with patience and humor, determination, optimism and love, the puzzle filled in and the pieces eventually came together and the effort was rewarded.

Ella and Baird had been rewarded.

Ella had a secret and she hadn't shared it with anyone yet, wanting Cara to hear it first. She made Baird swear not to tell Alec until Ella broke the news to her sister.

Carefully shifting sleeping Emma to the other arm, Ella reached into the tiny pocket on the front of her jeans, and slipped the diamond onto her fourth finger of her left hand, and then as casually as possible, she extended her hand to Cara. "What do you think?" she said, showing the ring off. "Do you approve?"

Cara grabbed her sister's hand, and held it tightly. "You're engaged?"

"You're the only one that knows." Ella smiled at Cara. "Baird is dying to tell Alec but I wanted to share with you first. None of this would have happened without you and that cottage." Her eyes filled with tears. "Oh, Cara, you're the best sister and friend. And now I'll just be living up the highway…four and a half hours. Not far at all."

Still cradling William, Cara jumped to her feet, and did a mad little dance. Everyone playing cricket turned to look. Ella saw Baird watching, too, and she raised her left arm in the air, showing off her ring hand.

Baird must have explained to Alec and the others because

suddenly they were all rushing toward them.

"When is the wedding?" Cara cried, as the family swarmed them.

Alec took his tiny daughter and Ella moved into Baird's arms. "When is the wedding?" she asked him, rising on tiptoe to kiss him.

He kissed her back and then looked around at everyone. "We were thinking a Christmas wedding."

"Yes! Oh, a Christmas wedding at Langley Park," Cara breathed, handing William to Alec, filling his arms. "It'd be gorgeous. We'd bring in a caterer and could open up the ballroom. It's a huge space—three rooms—with plenty of room for a dance floor and tables—"

"Darling, it's their wedding," Alec interrupted gently, but he was smiling. "But do consider the offer. You're family and we'd love to have you here, married at Langley Park, but obviously we will be wherever you tell us to be."

Baird and Ella exchanged glances. "We'd love to be married here," Ella said.

"If it didn't add too much chaos," Baird added. "We know December is already really busy here."

"Nothing would give us more happiness than to celebrate your love with us," Cara said firmly. "And if you sweet talk me a little bit, I'll persuade Alec to put you in the cottage for your wedding night. Honeymoon at the Cottage."

Everyone laughed and baby Emma stirred and began to cry. William opened his eyes but just looked around at everyone, so calm, so wise while Emma Eloise reminded everyone she was not going to be ignored.

Cara took Emma from Alec. Ella rose up to kiss Baird. The magic was real. Love at Langley Park.

The End

If you enjoyed *The Christmas Cottage*,
you'll love Book 1 in…

Love at Langley Park series

Book 1: *Once Upon a Christmas*

Book 2: *The Christmas Cottage*

Available now at your favorite online retailer!

Aunt Dorothy's Shortbread Cookies

Ingredients:

10 tbsp unsalted butter (if using salted butter, remove additional salt)

½ cup powder sugar

½ tsp pure vanilla extract

1 ½ cups all-purpose flour

½ tsp salt

Directions:

1. Beat the butter and sugar until creamed. Add vanilla extract and salt; beat until blended. Scrape the bowl down and add flour while beating on low. Scrape the bowl once more and mix until combined.
2. Shape the dough into a small flat loaf (rectangle), wrap in plastic and chill until firm.
3. Preheat the oven to 350*F. Use a sharp knife to cut half-inch thick slices. Place slices, spaced at least an inch apart, onto a greased baking sheet. Use a fork to indent a pattern into the cookies.
4. Bake for about 10 minutes. Transfer to a wire rack and cool.

The Eton Mess

Ingredients:

3 ½ – 4 cups strawberries, quartered, plus extra to serve

½ cup white granulated sugar or caster sugar

1 cup heavy whipping cream, lightly whisked

½ c crème fraiche (can skip and increase whipping cream by ½ c)

½ cup powdered sugar, sieved

½ tsp vanilla

½ – ¾ cup raspberries

Meringues

3 large egg whites

½ cup granulated sugar

½ cup powdered sugar, sieved

1 TBL corn flour

Directions:

1. For meringues, preheat oven to 250 F. Whisk egg white and a pinch of salt in an electric mixer until firm peaks form (3-4 minutes). With motor running, gradually add granulated sugar and whisk until thick and glossy (2-3 minutes). Sieve powdered sugar and corn flour over, fold to combine, then spoon 3-4 inch mounds onto oven trays lined with baking paper. Bake until meringues lift easily from trays and are crisp but not colored (45-50

minutes), then turn off the oven and cool completely in the oven.
2. Meanwhile, toss strawberries and granulated sugar in a large bowl to combine, then set aside until juices begin to seep (20 minutes).
3. Whisk cream, crème fraîche, powdered sugar, and vanilla in a separate large bowl until soft peaks form. Scatter a quarter of the strawberries in the base of a pretty large serving bowl, spread with a quarter of the cream mixture, and coarsely crumble a quarter of the meringue over the top. Repeat layering with the remaining ingredients.
4. Scatter Eton mess with raspberries, extra strawberries and serve!

More Books by Jane Porter

The Calhouns & Campbells of Cold Canyon Ranch series

Book 1: *Take Me Please, Cowboy!*

Book 2: *Bear's Heart*
Coming soon!

Book 3: *The Best Christmas*
Coming soon!

The Wyatt Brothers of Montana series

Book 1: *Montana Cowboy Romance*

Book 2: *Montana Cowboy Christmas*

Book 3: *Montana Cowboy Daddy*

Book 4: *Montana Cowboy Miracle*

Book 5: *Montana Cowboy Promise*

Book 6: *Montana Cowboy Bride*

Love on Chance Avenue series

Book 1: *Take Me, Cowboy*
Winner of the RITA® Award for Best Romance Novella

Book 2: *Miracle on Chance Avenue*

Book 3: *Take a Chance on Me*

Book 4: *Not Christmas Without You*

Paradise Valley Ranch series

Book 1: *Away in Montana*

Book 2: *Married in Montana*

The Taming of the Sheenans series

The Sheenans are six powerful wealthy brothers from Marietta, Montana. They are big, tough, rugged men, and as different as the Montana landscape.

Book 1: *Christmas at Copper Mountain*

Book 2: *The Tycoon's Kiss*

Book 3: *The Kidnapped Christmas Bride*

Book 4: *The Taming of the Bachelor*

Book 5: *A Christmas Miracle for Daisy*

Book 6: *The Lost Sheenan's Bride*

Other Titles

Oh, Christmas Night

The Tycoon's Forced Bride

The Frog Prince

Available now at your favorite online retailer!

About the Author

New York Times and USA Today bestselling author of 70 romances and fiction titles, **Jane Porter** has been a finalist for the prestigious RITA award six times and won in 2014 for Best Novella with her story, *Take Me, Cowboy*, from Tule Publishing. Today, Jane has over 13 million copies in print, including her wildly successful, *Flirting With Forty*, which was made into a Lifetime movie starring Heather Locklear, as well as *The Tycoon's Kiss* and *A Christmas Miracle for Daisy*, two Tule books which have been turned into holiday films for the GAC Family network. A mother of three sons, Jane holds an MA in Writing from the University of San Francisco and makes her home in sunny San Clemente, CA with her surfer husband and three dogs.

Thank you for reading

The Christmas Cottage

If you enjoyed this book, you can find more from all our great authors at TulePublishing.com, or from your favorite online retailer.

Made in the USA
Middletown, DE
17 December 2024